ALSO BY METTE NEWTH

The Abduction
The Dark Light

THE TRANSFORMATION

The Transformation

METTE NEWTH

TRANSLATED BY FAITH INGWERSEN

FARRAR, STRAUS AND GIROUX

NEW YORK

Farrar, Straus and Giroux
19 Union Square West, New York 10003

Copyright © 1997 by H. Aschehoug & Co.
Translation copyright © 2000 by Faith Ingwersen
Distributed in Canada by Douglas & McIntyre Ltd.
Printed in the United States of America
Designed by Judy Lanfredi
First published in 1997 by H. Aschehoug & Co.,
Norway, as *Forandringen*
First English-language edition published in 2000
by Farrar, Straus and Giroux
1 3 5 7 9 10 8 6 4 2

Library of Congress Cataloging-in-Publication Data
Newth, Mette.
    [Forandringen. English]
    The transformation / Mette Newth ; translated by Faith Ingwersen.—1st
English Language ed.
        p. cm.
    "First published in 1997 . . . as Forandringen"—T.p. verso.
    Summary: On a journey to appease the Sea's Mother, Navarana saves the
life of one of the strangers who had come to Greenland to rescue the
few Christians living there and together they find a way to end the suffering
of Navarana's people.
    ISBN 0-374-37752-9
    1. Inuit—Greenland—Juvenile fiction. [1. Inuit—Greenland—Fiction.
2. Eskimos—Greenland—Fiction. 3. Greenland—Fiction.] I. Ingwersen, Faith.
II. Title.

PZ7.N48665 Tr 2000
[Fic]—dc21   99-86323

EXCERPT FROM THE BULL OF POPE NICHOLAS V, on September 20, 1448, with a plea for rescue of the last Christians on Greenland:

Verily, concerning Our most beloved sons who are born and dwell throughout the island of Greenland . . . a sorrowful complaint has reached Our ear and has created bitterness in Our mind:

In the course of years, thanks to the eager piety of that island's population, numerous religious buildings, as well as a notable cathedral, have been erected. Mass was regularly performed until the day thirty years ago when . . . heathen barbarians, who had come across the ocean from nearby coasts, immigrated to the island and through their bloody attacks diminished the whole population living on the island and destroyed by fire and sword that people's fatherland and their sacred buildings. . . . And the unfortunate natives, men and women, . . . were abducted into slavery by the heathens to their own countries, just as they have been subjected to their tyrannical rule.

They have now brought before Us a humble plea that We should come to their rescue and paternally support their hope of salvation through Our benevolence and, by grace of the apostolic throne, fill the spiritual void into which they have been hurled.

THE TRANSFORMATION

ONE

"Navarana, you must not sleep too long."

The voice was near in her dream and as far away as the song of the whale. She scrambled quickly out of the igloo and saw that the early morning sky was blue and as open as hope and the Sea's Mother.

That was the sign she had waited for. Now she knew that the Sea's Mother would let her prey come. Perhaps this would also be the day when the sun regained its strength and ocean and land were again filled with life.

She turned her face toward the rim of the sky where the sun would rise, large and red, above the line of blue-black icebergs. She longed to sense the light glowing through her eyelids and to see the marvel of translucent icebergs once again sailing toward the edge of the world. Those colossal chunks of ice that the merciless cold had so long chained to the coast.

She waited with her eyes closed. On this day, when the sky was a wholly clear blue for the first time in ages, she must not abandon hope that the world would turn.

She clung to hope until there was no longer any doubt. But the rays were still cold against her skin, just as cold as they were on all the other mornings she had waited for the transformation. She opened her eyes. On the horizon the sun smoldered weakly and was quickly quenched by the frost haze. She saw the sky grow white and knew that the cold would be severe. This day, when the summer sun should have shone endlessly, winter would triumph. For three summers the unnatural winter had lasted, with a cold fiercer than anyone at the settlement could remember. With storms so violent that hunting along the coast was impossible. The people at the settlement had waited and hoped; they had sung songs and performed drum dances. But the sun always lost the battle. And the ice, which the storms had honed to a high polish, just grew thicker each day. The people had carefully followed the advice of the shaman to respect the taboos and live as the Sea's Mother wanted them to. Pitoraq, that mighty wind from the icy interior, rose up anyway. It forced them to stay inside while it filled valleys and hollows with powdery snow. Now they were growing increasingly anxious that the unnatural winter was a punishment that would never end.

No movement. No sound. Just threatening silence beneath a helpless sun.

Death moved one step closer.

She felt the frost that covered the earth's skin sift slowly through her own body. They were one, she and the land. The land would die without sun. Then she herself would die. The cold made joints stiffen and blood pump sluggishly through one's veins. This was a cold that not even her father's warm hunting outfit could protect her from.

Was it possible to freeze to death from disappointment?

In any case she must not sit and lose herself in disappointment. Even if the sun did not yet have the strength to rise, the Sea's Mother was still merciful to her. She had sent an animal as prey. It would prolong her own life and that of all the others at the settlement.

The animal had probably been waiting and was just as disappointed as she. It was also desperate from hunger, just as she was.

She got up with difficulty. Her trousers of shaggy polar-bear skin were covered with icicles that rattled softly as she stood up. The sound scraped at her ears, and she peered down at the dwellings of the strangers.

She had not dared to come so near before. But there was no avoiding it. The last hope was the fjord down below the strangers' settlement. All other hunting grounds along the coast were deserted and had been so for a long time. It was by the fjord that she had seen the bear clearly. Before she heard its voice.

The long winter had wreaked havoc on the strangers' settlement.

Serves them right, she thought bitterly. Maybe it was their fault. There was no other explanation. That was what many people thought.

The first time she saw the strangers' stone dwellings she was not afraid. But she had felt that they were unnatural. The dwellings loomed behind the stone fences as if the strangers owned the earth, the sheltered bay, and the sea beyond. But land and sea and air no one could own. All Human Beings knew that they only borrowed nature, just as their Ancestors had in their days on earth and just as their Descendants would in theirs.

The strangers could not have understood or cared about that. Perhaps nature had decided to reconquer what the strangers had taken. Therefore their settlement was drowned in snow, and the dwellings were sealed in thick sheaths of ice.

There could be no one alive at the strangers' now. Not after so long. She would have nothing to fear when she passed on her way to the fjord below.

The fjord, which once had been invitingly open, was now unnaturally full of thickly packed ice floes. Even the strong current could not manage to drive the masses of ice on toward the ocean, and they had frozen into frightening formations. Before, when everything was normal, the ice lay only along the shores of the blackish green fjord. Ice that was safe and enticing to playful seals and hungry hunters.

But the ice could be deceitful, she thought.

The ice let you believe that it was stable. Then it could suddenly break off and drift away with a father who, in a moment of unrestrained joy, had let his daughter try on his hunting outfit.

She had worn his outfit since that day when his eyes would not release hers, even after he had become invisible in the ice. She had expected him to rise up and fly to her, he who was invincible, he who could fly between all the known worlds. But there was only pain in his look, as if he had known that this was the way they were destined to part.

Perhaps that was the way it was destined. Just as with her mother. Or perhaps he had decided himself that he would follow her mother. Navarana would never know.

She must not think about it.

She brushed off her skin trousers with great care. The

icicles would clink much too loudly when she moved down toward the beach to see if her prey was waiting. She had learned now that one could never be too careful. Nothing in the world was certain. Only death.

The long anorak of shining silver sealskin presented no problem. Ice could not cling to its short hairs. The anorak fit her better than the trousers. They were much too large. But she would never be as tall as her father or ever stop missing him.

The *kamiks* made no noise. She had been careful to sew them so that her feet never lost their grip. They were made of sealskin and reached up to the middle of her thighs. She had lined them in the way that her grandmother who lived north of the great bay had taught her.

They should never have left her grandmother and the settlement in the north. Nothing had gotten better after that. Nothing. But her father could not be swayed, and she knew that he was too proud to stay.

"Hunger has already received our sacrifice," he merely said. "No one can demand more of us."

He who had been the most skilled hunter at the settlement had not been able to catch anything after her mother died. Maybe he had hoped that the game would return when he left. Because he left.

No one had stopped them when they loaded the long sled and the eager dogs started out across the ice in the bay toward Inuat Nuunat in the south. Inuat Nuunat—the Land of the Human Beings—with its mighty inland ice and long coast, ice-free and fertile in summer. The land that she imagined to be the white body of the Sea's Mother, resting between sky and sea.

"In the Land of the Human Beings we'll receive new hope," her father had said. "There our people have wandered from time immemorial. There they've always brought in a good harvest. Nowhere in the sea are the seals as plentiful or as fat. Never have you seen herds of reindeer as numerous and as well fed as on the plateau below the glacier."

But the winter, which was severe in the north, had become even more severe in the Land of the Human Beings, and it was at her relatives' settlement in the Land of the Human Beings that her father had lost his life.

She had decided to learn to use his hunting gear, so that she and her little sisters could survive. She asked the Old One for help.

"Hunger and terror make bad hunters," grumbled the Old One.

He was her grandmother's cousin and the person who had received them with the most kindness. He had taken care of her and her sisters after her father had disappeared. Navarana was ashamed of accepting food from the Old One, for she knew that he, too, was a burden to the families at the settlement. The fear that even he might be chased out had made her all the more determined to master her father's tools.

She had sat still for hours and practiced envisioning where the hare would hop up along the mountain slopes and where the shiny head of the seal would appear from the ice to breathe. She had tried to conjure the animals to her. She had sworn always to honor their souls, if only they would give their lives to her. But no hare or seal had let itself be enticed by her spells or stopped by her spear or harpoon. Always she had returned empty-handed to the settlement, and, ashamed, she had accepted bits of dried meat and blubber from the Old One.

As he offered her food, the Old One looked steadily at her in a way that was so like her grandmother's. And she understood that he knew that she did not have the power.

"I will manage," she usually said.

"Your father was a great hunter," he always answered.

She would not allow herself to be paralyzed by hopelessness. Maybe it was true that the lives of the Human Beings were determined by higher powers. But she refused to resign herself. All too much had just been left to destiny. She was going to try to change what was destined.

"Father wouldn't want me just to give up," she said one day, without knowing whether it was true.

"I wouldn't want that either. I am only saying that you mustn't let hunger and fear rule you. They bring no luck in hunting," he answered gently. "Remember that no one will chase you and your sisters from the settlement. It's still true, here among us, that *all* children are our children. That's just how it is. Your little sisters will have mothers here as long as we all can find a way. It's you I'm concerned about. But you will know when it's futile."

"I'll manage. I will!" she snapped.

"Few women have managed it."

"Enough of them!"

"True. But they were also great shamans."

After that she had decided to seek out the power that manifested itself in her dreams. In her dreams it had been formless and fleeting, and she always awakened with a feeling of loss. For in her dreams she had been united with a power that was endlessly greater and older than she.

She seated herself at the point of a deserted spit of land, far from the settlement, and kept a vigil and fasted for days and nights. Finally, one night, the power had assumed a shape and the bear became quite visible. She saw its huge shimmering body and felt that the breath from its open maw smelled sweet with blood. But she did not see its eyes. Eyes that she knew were as black and as deep as the death it wanted for her. And she knew that she had to want to live just as strongly as the bear wished her to die.

Convinced by the spirit vision, she began to train with her father's heavy bear spear. She chose a block of ice that was the same size as her bear. She practiced for many days, until she was confident that the spear lay steadily in her hand, and she hit the middle of what would have been the bear's chest. Again she fasted and kept a vigil for nights and days, until she envisioned the place where their trial of strength was to be fought out.

Then she went to the Old One to tell him that she had seen the grassy hillock with the looming stone dwellings beneath the main mountain range at the end of the fjord. She did not say that she saw the bear spring wildly at her.

"Yes, now you've *seen* your power, but have you met the bear's gaze?"

She hesitated before she shook her head no.

"Then you should wait a little longer."

But she dared not wait, even if it had not shown her its *Inua*, its soul. It could change its mind. Not wait for a test of strength with her.

"I don't like your seeing it by the strangers' settlement."
He was obviously worried. "Though they may be ever so
dead, we don't know what has happened to their souls.
Dangerous spirits may be wreaking havoc there. In any
case, they're not *our* spirit guides."

"Think of all the food the bear will give us."

"You'll not allow yourself to be stopped?"

"I know of nothing that can stop me now," she had answered.

Her fear, she had tried to suppress. But it had returned as
she crawled up the slippery mountain gorge and heard
Pitoraq. The wind ruled many evil spirits, and now they were
all howling toward her. Fear had racked her ever since she
saw the fjord and the strangers' frozen dwellings and had
built the little igloo and lay in wait there for the bear. She
was scared to meet the bear and scared that it would not
come. Most of all she feared the strangers' hungry spirits,
which might not have left the dead settlement. But she endured night and day while Pitoraq raged. For she could not
give up the struggle against what was perhaps her destiny.

She did not see it at once, even though she was standing
up.

It must have lain behind the strangers' small dwelling at
the edge of the beach, the one that she had first believed to

be a large snow-covered rock. Now the bear was standing on its hind legs, and she saw that it was taller than a full-grown man. Its size did not frighten her. She was just grateful that it had waited and wanted to measure its strength against hers. She dared not imagine that she would win. If she lost, the bear would still fill in whatever was missing in her dream. That was not frightening either. For she herself had decided on the battle with the bear, and perhaps she could manage what no one else dared to try: to change what was destined to be.

She took a step forward. The spear lay securely in her hand.

Snarling, the bear lifted one of its forepaws and struck. The blow made the foreign dwelling shake, and the sod roof appeared from beneath the snow.

"*Aia*! Are you trying to frighten me? *Aia*! Just let me at you!"

She took some steps forward.

The bear roared, turned sharply, and threw itself on something that lay frozen down between the stones on the shore. She could not see what it was, but she heard wood splintering beneath the bear's violent blows. Whatever it had been, it no longer was.

She leapt down across the slope and felt laughter bubbling up in her throat. It was peculiar. The enraged bear ought to have paralyzed her. But it did not do so. On the contrary, she was filled with a confidence the like of which she had never known before.

She stopped some spear lengths from the bear. She was just near enough to put weight in the throw, just far enough away not to be struck by the sharp claws of a forepaw when the bear quickly turned and went on the attack.

She waited.

But the massive animal stayed facing the other way. Its lowered head moved slowly from side to side as it sniffed the air in her direction.

She lifted the spear and stared.

How handsome it was. But so terribly thin. All too clearly she saw the powerful muscles and the black skin beneath its coat. The long, yellowish white hair moving in rhythm with the bear's breath reminded her of seaweed swaying in the sea.

She stamped her feet lightly.

It was dangerous. The bear could hurl itself on her before she managed to thrust the spear into its breast. But she had to make it turn around.

"*Aia!*" she sang. "Mighty Sister, I am not a worthy adversary for you! Still, let me take your life in fair combat and I promise to care for your soul as if it were my own."

She readied herself for the death thrust.

The bear turned, slowly, hesitantly, and she saw its breast, that huge breast where its coat parted into fine waves around a large, red, open sore.

Horrified, she let the spear sink. She had dreamt about this fatal wound. She just did not know that it was the bear's wound that she had seen.

The bear lifted its forepaws.

Instinctively, she lifted the spear and took a step closer.

But the bear made no motion to approach her.

Then she saw that it was a sow. Fortunately, it was not with young.

For a long time they both waited uncertainly. Quietly. Both looked up at the same time. When their eyes met, she saw death lying deep in the sow's eyes.

"You *are* my soul," she whispered. "Your *Inua* shall be within me and hunt with me. Always."

Carefully, almost tenderly, she let the spear point rest against the gaping wound.

The sow's eyes did not leave hers.

"I shall never forget that you gave your life, Sister. Soon you will be going home to rest with the Sea's Mother. I shall bury the corners of your mouth in the earth beneath the snow and turn your head toward the sea. I shall honor your soul. One day you will see that I am worthy of you as my spirit guide."

She stabbed quick and hard with all her strength.

The blood spurted warmly right at her.

The sow gave no resistance. She remained standing until her eyes grew dull and empty. Then she sank. Slowly.

Navarana quickly drew the spear out of the sow's heart, even though it could no longer harm the bear. Then she lay down against its warm throat and cried for a long time.

TWO

Be still!

The crescent-shaped knife had to lie steady in her hand. But her hand refused to obey.

The *ulo* was the women's knife. It had been her mother's pride, as it was hers. The *ulo* had served her faithfully ever since she had first been allowed to help the women flay the game that the hunters brought home. Now it would not lie still, just as the wind, Pitoraq, warned that it was coming with all its spirits.

Her exhaustion must not get the better of her. Not now, when the worst part was over. To sever the bear's head from its body was work for at least two people, but she had managed it alone. Never had anything been more difficult than cutting the bear's throat and powerful neck muscles. It was as if she were cutting into herself. Never would she forget the sound of the vertebrae in the neck as they reluctantly slid apart.

Her stomach was in a painful knot as she placed the sow's head on the snowless stone. Not until the dead eyes looked out at what had been the sow's hunting grounds did the cramps lose their grip on her. By then she was so exhausted that she scarcely managed to place one of her father's bear claws at the back of the sow's throat.

The sow shall have Father's strongest amulet just to make sure, she had thought, even though she knew that the sow and she would meet again anyway. Her father had given her two claws from the first bear he had felled. It had been a strong and proud male bear, and a long time had passed before it appeared as his spirit guide. Its claws had a strong magical power, her father had said. Navarana had always carried the claws in the medicine pouch on her chest. Now she cut the snout off her sow and put it in the medicine pouch with the remaining bear claw. It would be her most powerful protection. Finally she hacked out a hollow in the frozen earth, deep enough for the corners of the bear's mouth to rest in peace. Not until then was she satisfied that everything had been done in the proper way to free the sow's soul. She could then begin the slow work of flaying and cutting up the heavy body.

"Please, there is so little time," she pleaded.

But her hand refused to hold the *ulo* steady.

She saw the heavy fog bank glide across the ice. It devoured the landscape greedily. Soon the storm and the fog would merge and she would become blind and helpless.

Time was short, but everything had to be right. The pelt that the sow had given her could not receive the tiniest gash. The *ulo* had to be steady so that the cutting of that beautiful hide would be completely straight. Then the hide had to be parted from the flesh and all the meat cut and packed. Not until that was done could she find shelter from the storm.

She commanded herself to sit still and to concentrate on making the first slash.

Perhaps it was the sow's power that steered the knife in a straight slash from neck to belly. Certainly it did not happen through her own willpower. That had been spent long before.

Gratefully, she licked the warm animal blood from her frozen hands. Then she continued to cut the skin loose from the huge thighs and forepaws as quickly as she dared.

The storm would not wait any longer. Pitoraq's demons showed no mercy, she knew. They were already howling, and she recognized the sharp odor of deadly frost. Needles of ice burned against her bare cheeks.

She had to seek shelter, but she could not do so until the meat was securely hidden. It would be safe down by the fjord between the large stones on the shore. Even though she had not seen the greedy wolf for a long time, she would cover it with blocks of ice. She would pack as much meat as she could carry in the hide, knowing that everyone at the settlement was as starved as she. She knew that the demons would do everything in their power to stop her. But she could not let herself be stopped now, for she would gain new strength from the bear's heart.

While she ate the sow's still-warm heart, she thought about the bear's journey. Perhaps the sow had already reached the Sea's Mother. In that blue dwelling there was more than enough room for all Her children.

At last most of the bear carcass was safely hidden and the rest packed in the hide. With satisfaction she saw that the hide had not gotten a single gash. She looked forward to tanning and treating it. It would be her most precious possession.

Then she no longer had the strength to hold off her exhaustion.

"Don't sleep now," she said aloud.

That was the last thing she remembered.

Suddenly she was awakened by a violent blow to her chest. She had been tossed against one of the pointed stones of the shore. She clung to the stone in order not to be swept out on the fjord ice.

The polar-bear skin! That greedy Pitoraq had taken her bundle!

She was blind in the dense blizzard. Her tears froze to ice on her cheeks as she fumbled in the drifts of loose new snow. It was hopeless to search for it now, but she knew that terror would overcome her if she did not continue. The sow was not to have helped her in vain.

Pitoraq, who had thrown her down among the stones with such force, could have driven her bundle far away. She scrabbled on. With fingers that no longer felt like her own, she investigated each stone. Suddenly she bumped against a wall of ice. It was the strangers' small wooden dwelling, the one that had been completely covered by snow when the bear attacked it. At the time she had considered seeking shelter in the dwelling if the storm grew too bad. She had not imagined that the opening would be blocked by thick ice.

For some time she sat leaning up against the ice wall that separated her from safety.

"I will not give up now!"

She could scarcely hear her own shout above the storm.

Warmth. She had to get her blood to flow swiftly through her veins again. She took off her mittens and *kamiks* and massaged her hands and feet with snow, rocking quickly back and forth, trying to ignore the pain.

Where had Pitoraq driven her bundle? It could have drifted off anywhere, since the demons came swirling from all directions. They would pursue her to her death if she did not carefully choose where to search.

"Aia, Big Sister. Aia! Help me live so I can show myself to be worthy of your power."

She continued to sing until her words turned into certainty. Then she started to scrabble toward the pieces of wood that stuck up from the ice of the fjord. She saw that they were thin, round poles. They had certainly belonged to the strangers. The poles had the fresh marks of sharp claws. Here the sow had searched for food. She had smashed the wood into splinters. Obviously she had not found anything to eat.

Navarana knew that she ought to crawl by. The place was extremely sinister, but it was here the sow had stopped. So she must dare to do the same. She began to dig the snow away along the remains of the poles. Soon she saw the outline of something large and oblong, a shape resembling the women's boats that the whalers in the north used, only much larger. She knew she had found the strangers' boat. Had it lain by the beach when the fjord froze solid? Had the strangers forgotten to pull their boat onto land when the terrible winter arrived? Or had they perhaps all been dead already?

She stood up quickly, her heart racing.

Were the strangers lying under the ice in wait for a living person? Was that why the sow had tried to destroy the boat?

She shivered, but not from the cold.

She knew nothing about the strangers. Everything the people at the settlement told of them was frightening. The strangers were gigantic, it was said, much larger than any Human Being, and they looked terrible. Their skin and hair were unnaturally pale, and the men had a lot of hair on their faces. They are as shaggy as musk oxen, someone had said and laughed. But no one laughed at the strangers' long knives, which were not of bone or stone. And no one could explain why the strangers kept animals trapped in the dwellings or behind stone fences. It was completely unnatural to keep captive animals that were not sled dogs. And no one had seen sleds there. It was said that the strangers' animals were also very odd. Some were larger than reindeer and had sharp horns. Some were smaller with thick, curly coats. The very oddest animals were larger than reindeer and without horns. They had smooth coats and shag only on their necks, and their tails were long and resembled human hair. The strangers sat on the backs of these animals. No one had ever seen anything odder.

It had been ages since anyone had dared to visit the

strangers' settlement. Navarana had seen it only once, and then from a safe distance.

The Old One had told of a time when the Human Beings visited the strangers and peacefully bartered meat and skins. The evidence was at the Human Beings' settlement. She had seen wooden pots and ladles that no Human Being had made. But something had happened that was so terrible that not even the Old One would talk about it. After that no one had approached the strangers, for everyone knew that fear brings enmity and death. This had happened often enough during the history of Human Beings. It had always led to families being wiped out or whole settlements laid waste.

For the first time during this whole exhausting day she felt that terror would paralyze her.

Human Beings knew little of the life of the strangers, she thought. They knew even less about the strangers' death. Still, even if their restless souls were waiting beneath the ice, she had no other choice than to follow the sow's tracks. But she hesitated a long time before she scrabbled in among the remains of that scary boat.

The discovery came as a complete surprise. The heavy bundle lay in what had been the stern of the boat, and she knew that the sow was satisfied with her.

"Mighty Sister!" she shouted. "Thanks to you I can overcome anything!"

And it was true. For she alone would not have had the
strength to drag that heavy bundle up the slippery bank
from the shore. When she reached the top, she saw that
the open plain was a churning sea of snow. She fell to her
knees before Pitoraq managed to knock her down. It was
impossible to get home to those who were waiting for food.
Even great spirit guides bowed down before Pitoraq. And
people had to do so, too. Submit and endure in order to
survive, but never lose hope. Never stop struggling to
change things.

The murky yellow daylight would soon darken. She had
to find shelter before the deadly cold of night. There was
nothing on the plain with which to build an igloo. To bury
oneself in loose snow was too dangerous. You would either
freeze or choke to death.

She could not see the strangers' dwellings through the
blizzard, but she knew where they lay and that there were
many of them. It ought to be possible to find shelter in one
of them. She could manage to scrabble there. If she dared.

She had to dare. She who had conquered the sow and
been aided by the sow's power would be safe in the
strangers' dwellings until the storm abated.

The wind's demons did all they could to prevent her
from scrabbling on, and she felt that her fear of the un-

known was stronger than her will. She was not angry at Pitoraq, for he was only doing what he had to do. It was her own fear that infuriated her. It would paralyze her and abandon her to the storm.

She did not see the dwelling before she stumbled on it. Then she understood that the sow had helped her yet again. The opening lay leeward to the wind, and the wooden plank stood ajar, enough for her to be able to squeeze by.

She listened warily in the alien darkness. Even through the howling storm she heard the silence of the room. It did not seem threatening.

She sniffed.

The odor that pricked her nose was unidentifiable and musty, but she recognized no odor of a being, either living or dead. She ought to have investigated whether something was still lurking in the dark, but she was too exhausted. Besides, she knew that what you feel with your hands at night is much worse than what you see with your eyes in daylight.

It was cold here. Just as cold as outside. But at least the stone walls kept the wind out, and her whale-oil lamp would give warmth. She decided to sleep in the bearskin without her clothes. That would give her a feeling of greater safety as she slept.

When she had finished easing the meat out of the hide,

she cut off a piece of the sow's liver and chewed morsels slowly and painstakingly. It was dangerous to eat quickly when one had gone hungry for a long period. There were also those who thought that polar-bear liver was something one had to be careful of. But her sow's liver tasted neither harsh nor poisonous. It tasted wonderful, and the slow chewing made her sleepy.

Why on earth did they live among stones? It was incomprehensible that the strangers, as long as they had been in this land, had not learned to build as the Human Beings did. The dwellings of the Human Beings always lay sheltered and warm, half-buried in the ground, with long subterranean entryways that kept the cold at a safe distance. All sensible people knew that naked stones preserved the cold, whereas earth and sod and stone together preserved the heat. Anyway, she was much too tired to worry about something to which she would get no answer. She curled up in the polar-bear skin.

She missed the stories that provided safe dreams and the naked bodies that provided heat for one another. No one froze from loneliness in the dwellings of the Human Beings. But she was not lonely anyway, for as soon as she closed her eyes, she saw the bear. It flew toward her through blue space. In its wide embrace she clearly saw its

fatal wound. She knew that one day, when her apprenticeship as a shaman was at an end, the sow would show her its
soul in the wound. She would see a beautiful soul shining
white as the sow itself, and strong, for it would be half bear
and half Human Being. On the day that the sow offered to
be her spirit guide she would no longer be afraid to try to
change that which everyone called destiny.

THREE

She woke reluctantly from a dream in which the spring rain was falling softly on her face in the heather. Great golden drops that mirrored fluttering butterflies and the sun's enormous rainbow across the sky.

She could not bear waking up to the colorless light and the storm's continued raging. Pitoraq would not let her return home to those who were waiting today, either. She could hear it in the gusts of wind outside. She just wanted to dream on about all the beautiful things that the great frost had stolen. In her dream the world was as it ought to be. She heard the hoarse shrieks of the geese announcing that summer was on its way. She saw the cormorants crowding together in the evening sun's last rays before the ice floe they were sitting on slipped into the shadow of night. She felt the heart of the downy chick beating furiously in her hands and tasted freshly slaughtered seal in her mouth. All that wonderful life the winter had stolen. Now it could be found only in dreams and stories.

Navarana had asked the Old One if the endless winter was the strangers' fault.

"It's easy just to blame others. But that makes you blind to your own failings." And he had warned her against losing herself in dreams.

"I know that dreams don't fill the stomach, but at least they keep hope alive," she had answered and immediately regretted it. The Old One was extremely stern but he was right, and of course she knew that. She had often been annoyed that the hunters wasted their time complaining about the strangers and dreaming about earlier successful hunts rather than trying to transform what was destined to be.

"Forgive me, Master. I know you're right."

He had gazed at her for a long time from beneath his bushy brows, which were still as black as a raven's wings. "You shouldn't just obey me. You must think for yourself, right or wrong, but the thoughts and experiences must be your own. Only then will I know that you can become a good shaman. Think about it, Navarana, do you believe the Sea's Mother will be satisfied by our dreams? Can She trust our promises never again to break Her taboos?"

She shook her head no.

"She wants us to assume responsibility for our own lives," he said sternly. "Not just shove blame onto others."

It was the first time anyone had told her that it was possible to change what the Sea's Mother or the Raven had predetermined.

"What can I do?" she had asked.

He laughed. The tiny shells in his hair rustled with a whispering sound reminiscent of sun-baked sand. "At any rate you should stay as stubborn as you are now. If you endure, you may find the right path."

It was then that she understood that her quest was important to them all.

It was not possible to go back to sleep. She rose from the warm bearskin and felt the cold stinging her naked skin. Quickly she pulled on her skin undergarment. She had caught the eider ducks herself, and it had been a test of her patience to cut and sew the small pieces from their breasts. Now she was glad for having made the effort, for cold and dampness glanced off the eider duck, and nothing warmed the body as quickly as the down of its breast. Her inner trousers and stockings of hare skin were white with frost, and she regretted that she had not slept with her clothes on.

As soon as she was dressed, she began to investigate the square room.

It was empty, except for a large wooden vessel, which she was not able to lift, and some small broken objects, which she did not recognize. She held the well-polished objects in her hands for some time and sensed that they were quite dead. No alien spirits were protecting them. This she was certain of, but she didn't know whether she was relieved or disappointed. It was peculiar that there was no living trace of the strangers here. She grew more curious to investigate their settlement. Perhaps she would find answers to the questions that no one at home could answer. The mystery that kept them in fear of the strangers' returning in vengeance.

"Curiosity will be the death of you," her father had once said, laughingly.

"But isn't curiosity the best way to learn?" she answered innocently, and both knew that the answer was not that simple.

"Curiosity and caution are brother and sister," he said. "They must always go hand in hand."

Now she knew that he had been right, for it had been her curiosity that had taken him out onto the ice floe where his caution had failed him.

Outside, the sun was a pale yellow shadow on the rim of the white sky. It was no longer snowing. But Pitoraq had risen from the inland ice with renewed strength, and he now chased sky-high swirls of snow around the strangers' dwellings.

His white-clad, dancing demons, she thought. They are alluringly beautiful and dangerous.

For a long time she studied the demons' dance. She took note of how often the squalls came, from which direction they were coming, and how fast the demons turned. As long as Pitoraq used such might, it was futile to believe that she would reach home safely.

There were as many dwellings as the fingers on both her hands. The largest was larger than any of the Human Beings' dwellings. She had slept in the one that was smallest. The oddest dwelling stood a little apart. Its roof pointed threateningly at the sky. She was not sure she dared visit it.

She investigated the dwellings thoroughly. She saw equipment, work tools, and objects they could make use of at home, even if most of them were broken. But she took nothing. It was eerie that the strangers had left so much behind. What kind of people left equipment that could easily be repaired? She knew of no one so negligent.

Not even the strangers could be like that, she thought uneasily. The feeling of being close to a great tragedy grew more and more insistent. If only there had been a trace of a battle or of violent death! But the rooms were mute concerning the strangers' fate. Everywhere an oppressive, cold silence reigned, as if time had long been frozen. Everything was orderly. As if someone was expected to return. Or had carefully prepared for his final journey.

She was relieved when she saw the stiffly frozen animal carcass. It immediately made everything seem normal, even though the carcass she had found was of one of those strange foreign animals. Even though its coat was badly mangled and the flesh had been brutally ripped from its bones.

It was evident that many people had eaten and slept in the largest dwelling. She had not expected to find living creatures, but neither had she expected to see so clearly that the strangers had left the settlement in great haste. She saw a bowl that had the remains of food at the bottom and an upended pot. On the benches she saw candles that had gone out and a shining cross on a ripped-off chain. Immediately the feeling of misfortune grew strong and close, and she no longer wished to discover what had interrupted the meal here. She only wanted to get out, fast.

The smell of snow and frozen sea was liberating after that confined eeriness.

It was wrong to be here. She was certain. Wrong and perhaps dangerous. Who knew what powers of enchantment the dead strangers still had?

She would hide in the bearskin and dream until the storm stilled. But she could not keep her eyes off the dwelling with the peculiar roof and the smooth walls. It was, she thought, like a face without eyes, both repelling and enticing. She could not see the opening. It was hidden beneath high snowdrifts. She didn't see it until she was quite close. The feeling of being an intruder was strong. It grew stronger as she dug out the opening and discovered that the heavy wooden plank would not budge.

"Won't disturb you," she mumbled. "I just have to know what you're concealing."

She had to use all her strength to pull away the wooden plank.

Blinded by the darkness and her terror, she did not see the light at first. Slowly, the darkness became slightly gray and she saw light seeping in from the roof high above, filling half the room. Light running along the icicles hanging from the holes in the roof, light sparkling like stars on the frozen walls, light dancing in cobweb-fragile bridges of ice. A play of ice and light so enchanting that her flesh turned to goose bumps and she longed for the icebergs' green-gleaming caverns.

The room was bare and silent, but the silence was different from that in the other dwellings. In the deepest darkness something knew she was there. Something that had a look that was so vivid that she sensed it speaking. She would have run, but her legs refused to support her.

She closed her eyes and waited. But nothing happened, and she dared to meet that look again. It was neither evil nor disdainful. Slowly, she walked through the darkness and saw it clearly, a wooden figure on the wall.

It was a portrayal of a stranger, she was sure of it. The hair was light-colored, the skin white, and the body was long and slim. Different from a Human Being's and still amazingly similar. The figure's arms were outstretched, and its hands and feet were nailed to two planks laid crosswise. The head with that vivid look was slightly bowed, but she clearly saw the deep furrows of pain around the mouth. Dark streaks ran from the hands, feet, and eyes, and she understood that they represented blood. Blood that ran and ran, while the figure suffered for all eternity. It was disgusting.

What kind of people had they been to depict themselves in such pain, when life itself was so painful? She was suddenly terribly frightened. The figure was perhaps a *tupilaq*, a cruel avenger sent by the strangers' sorcerers to strike anyone who dared to enter here. Or was it a fatal trap that the Raven had laid to prevent her from changing what he had decided?

She had to get out. Perhaps the sow's power was not strong enough against this peril.

Then she heard the sound. Like the whimper of a child who does not have the strength to cry.

The sound came from the farthest stone in the darkness.

Her hands turned ice-cold as she stood thinking.

It *was* a trap. The Avenger or the Raven would lure her to them with a child's whimpering prayer for help. But it *could* really be a child. She knew that if she did not help she would always hear those desperate prayers in her dreams.

She clutched the medicine pouch with the sow's snout and her father's bear claw. Slowly, her fingertips grew warm, and she sensed the flow of power. No power in the world was stronger than that which had helped her through the storm. The sow bade her continue. The sow wanted her protected one to protect others.

She leaned into the darkness. Her fantasy conjured up devilish pictures of what she would have to endure meeting behind the block of stone.

A figure was lying there. A lifeless figure with arms outstretched and palms turned up exactly like the figure on the wall. But this figure was not of wood. It was of flesh and blood.

For the first time she was seeing one of the mysterious strangers. She stared and gasped.

It could not be accidental. That light-colored hair, long and sleek, was precisely the same color as the sow's coat. The face and hands shone like the moon, cool and distant. She saw fine down around the narrow mouth and on the chin. Down the same magic color as the hair. It was a young male. Maybe only a little older than she. There was a purpose to this, but it was hidden from her.

The stranger was terribly thin. He must have gone hungry for a very long time, but his face was peaceful, without a trace of suffering.

As if his struggle for life had ended, she thought.

She waited, but she saw no sign of life in his face. It was impossible to see whether he was breathing beneath the stiff clothing that covered his body from throat to foot.

Had she imagined the sounds?

Cautiously, she laid her fingers on his blue lips and felt a slight breath. No, he was not dead, but his breath smelled of death. It would not be long before his soul left for the Land of the Dead.

"I shouldn't be here then!"

She quickly rose.

At the same moment he opened his eyes, and in them she stared at a will so strong that it could have been her own. His eyes were as clear and as blue as the summer sky.

FOUR

Slowly the light was vanishing, the unique light that had made the heavenly splendor quite apparent to him. Light fragrant with lavender and honeysuckle and vibrant with the angels' paeans to God, the Almighty Creator. He had felt the light pull out of him and fold in upon itself. He had seen it shrink to a cold star in endless space, and he had begged to be allowed to accompany it.

Then the golden voice had spoken: "Weep not, Brendan. You who have been allowed to see what awaits the unfaithful in hell's burning darkness. You whom I have allowed to view heaven's eternal joy. Have you still not understood the meaning of your vision? Have you still not seen the goal of your journey and your task on earth?"

The angel's voice was as sad as a final good-bye. The radiance disappeared with the voice. The darkness of night grew colder around him, he who was not yet allowed to follow along to that eternal bliss.

He fought against waking up. If only he could dream on, he would perhaps get another chance to be in the light. He did not fear the hunger and pain that would harry his body or the demons that unceasingly hammered in his head and against the church's walls. He feared only the absence of the all-encompassing light. That which had turned death in this inhospitable land into a profound expectation.

Lord Christ, did you have to let me return?

In the gray light from the cracks in the roof His face was impassive. Never had he seen it so encrusted with ice, and suddenly he was filled with fear. Maybe God had yielded this hell on earth to the Devil after all!

The thought was monstrous, and he realized immediately that it was his sinful soul speaking. His soul that had fled from the struggle that had cost the lives of so many courageous brothers. The struggle that was now his alone.

"*Mea culpa . . . Confiteor Deo omnipotenti . . .* Lord! Forgive my sinful deeds. *Mea maxima culpa.* Almighty Father, You who let Your Son die on the cross for our sakes. Creator of all life. You who shall judge the living and the dead.

Never would You yield to the Devil. Never . . ." The prayer streamed out in a confused mixture of the Holy Church's language and his childhood's Celtic.

He was deeply ashamed of his soul's cowardice and his body's weakness, of his longing for people and his longing for the light's blessing. For he who had been chosen to do battle for the soul's salvation in the farthest reaches of the world had failed. He did not possess faith's unconquerable strength in the way the abbot had hoped and he himself in his arrogance had believed. He had not come to this hell of ice and storms to serve the Lord. He had come to fulfill his own most secret dream. It was his own eternal bliss he had sought, not God's mercy for the unfortunate Northmen. He had been consumed with purifying himself through fasting and prayer, not with battling the terrible harryings of death. He had told himself that it was the ailing brothers he watched over and prayed so intensely for. But it was all a shameful lie.

"*Mea maxima culpa* . . . Lord, look with mercy upon Your errant servant. I have sinned and repent of my sins."

He suddenly fell silent, for he also knew that his prayer was false. He had not gone astray at all. He had carefully planned each painful step toward that deep sleep and ecstasy. He had been blind with arrogance, that was true. But not even his repentance was real. For he was still drunk with triumph over the fact that he, the most wretched of Saint Augustine's order, had been so near the vision, the vision that only the most saintly of men experience.

Forgiveness of sin, only the pure of heart receive!

It was not Christ's voice he heard. It was his own conscience.

Look within yourself to seek the source of your reckless selfishness. Not until your repentance is genuine and you have submitted to God's will, will He look upon you with mercy.

"Heavenly Father, chastise me as I deserve, but give me the strength to live and atone for my sins!"

In his heart it sounded like a cry, but he heard it as the pitiful whimper of a child. But if only God's ear was open, he would perhaps be heard. He remembered clearly the day that he had understood that his dream of a vision journey could come true.

It was a perfect day, infused with sun-warmed lavender and honeysuckle, as he floated in easy bounds between heaven and earth. On that day he was happy as a child, since God's smile filled the morning light and he knew that the moment was uniquely his. In the oak forest's deep shadows he had taken off his clothes and embraced the ground. As the honeysuckle's petals fell against his skin, he had promised always to remember that day. It was the day that he was to begin his journey across the sea to the Holy Church's last outpost in Greenland.

The ship had lain some time by the beach, awaiting the Augustinian brothers. The steersman's sharp drumbeat signaled the crew's impatience to set sail. The crew was accustomed to the long voyage across the stormy Northwest Sea and knew that it was one of the most dangerous passages in the world. But the little flock of robe-clad monks, who had wandered here from all parts of England to serve the Lord in distant Greenland, still knelt, absorbed in prayer, on the smooth stones of the shore.

As for himself, he had thanked the Lord sincerely for his being called, for finally he saw a sign that he was to follow in the footsteps of Saint Brendan, the holy man after whom he was named. They were of the same ancient lineage, Saint Brendan and he, but separated by many centuries. As a child he had listened eagerly to accounts of the courageous monk's perilous voyage toward northern lands and islands that no one had seen before. Saint Brendan's horrendous experiences and miraculous deliverance had consoled him when he was carted off from the little hamlet on Ireland's coast and sold to the monastery in Hereford. At the monastery the dream had received renewed sustenance when he learned to read, for Brother Gareth, a librarian who himself had been abducted from Ireland, had let him study Saint Brendan's own account.

"Diligence like yours is seldom found among the young," Brother Gareth had said.

"I burn to serve the Lord and to perform His miracles," he answered, happy that he could learn everything about the trials Saint Brendan had had to suffer. It had not for a moment occurred to him to doubt whether his solemn words were true. He longed merely for a chance to prove that he could tolerate just as much as that holy monk.

When the abbot called the monks to him and told them that the Holy Father in Rome had sent a bull to the bishops on Iceland with an urgent prayer for their help for the unfortunate Christians on Greenland, Brendan knew that his dream would come to pass. The description that Pope Nicholas had given of the fate that had befallen the population on Greenland had touched all the brothers deeply. The inhabitants had not only suffered long from hunger and illness through raging storms and bitter cold but also been subject to prolonged attacks and enslavement by heathen pirates.

When the abbot proclaimed that the monastery would follow God's call by sending priests and monks to save the Holy Church's farthest outpost, Brendan was among the first to beg the abbot to let him serve the Lord on Greenland.

The voyage across the ice-filled ocean was more dreadful than he had imagined but it did not frighten him. Rather he was strengthened in his conviction that these trials were similar to those Saint Brendan had had to withstand. As one brother after another fell victim to seasickness, he had stood in the bow praying. Unceasingly and sincerely he prayed, and at last the towering waves had stilled, the mountains of ice had opened, and the tiny vessel was cast into the harbor at Herjolfsnes, on the southern point of that wild land.

He had been the first to fall to his knees on the frozen beach and praise God for his salvation.

But he and the brothers had soon begun wondering what God's intention could be in sending them to Greenland. Not only were the monasteries of Saint Olaf and Saint Augustine closed to one and all by enormous masses of ice, but the bishop's residence at Gardar and the farms along the outlying fjords also lay deserted. For weeks they had sailed along the eastern settlement, Austerbygd, trying to enter the fjords to look for Christians. For an equally long period they had sailed along the rugged coast of the western settlement, Vesterbygd. Never had they seen such isolation as in these small scattered settlements and never such hopelessness as that among the few people who were still alive. The misfortune that reigned everywhere soon set its mark on the brothers. They who had lived so long in such safety in the monasteries in fertile England did not have the strength to resist illness and hopelessness, hunger and cold in this harsh land. Brendan realized that he might soon be alone if the brothers did not regain their belief in the holy mission they were to carry out here. He himself was certain that God had chosen him for a task far greater than that of saving a handful of souls, for he was ever more convinced that Satan was ravaging the land.

He had asked the helmsman if it was so. He gruffly answered that this heathen land had always been harsh and had never been populous. But still the Northmen had lived here for several hundred years and had cultivated the earth in the way they were accustomed to in Norway and Iceland. Then this endless winter had arrived. Combined with bloody feuds and attacks by barbaric pirates, it had finally broken the Northmen or driven them to flight.

"The Holy Father in Rome is rather late with his rescue. He should've heard their prayers many years ago, while there was still hope," the helmsman had said angrily.

Brendan had listened sympathetically while his conviction turned to unshakable certainty. It was here in this doomed land that God had determined that he should begin his great journey toward eternal salvation. He had consoled the sick and his discouraged brothers and said that there still was hope of finding souls to save. Then he had asked the helmsman to put them ashore at the far end of the longest fjord in Vesterbygd. The helmsman had warned against it. The fjord could become filled with ice at any time, and then the monks would be doomed. But he allowed himself to be convinced, for Brendan was ardent in the belief that God was holding His hand over them and would allow miracles to occur.

"Lord, how I have failed You and the brothers and all those You sent me to save!" For the first time he understood that his failure was irredeemable. No penitent prayers could change what he had done.

"Do not forsake me!" He cried like a child begging a father for one last chance. "I am nothing without Your mercy!"

But God was absent.

Perhaps His ear was just turned somewhere else? Brendan searched for the thin thread of light.

At the outermost edge of his consciousness there was a scraping sound. He strained to hear, and the sound grew. It was of something close and soft, and he knew that it was wary. He recognized the rank odor of a wild animal.

All at once it was completely clear what God wanted of him, and his answer rang in his head: Yes! I shall combat the devil and put an end to all his evil ways. This earthly realm shall also be Yours for all eternity!

He saw only the black gleaming hair, and he was relieved

that he avoided seeing that terrible face, half-animal, half-human. It scrabbled quickly toward him on all fours, and he saw the lithe movements of its body beneath its fur.

"Get thee hence, Satan!" he gasped.

But it was too late. It was already leaning over him. Its breath near his chin stank of warm blood. There was blood on the black hand touching his lips. Darkness enclosed him as soon as he met those black eyes with their glint of gold.

FIVE

Time trickled slowly by as Navarana waited.

He had been unconscious for quite some time. She still saw only the whites of his eyes, covered by fine red blood vessels. He was far away, but not out of his body. His thin hands twitched slightly, and he gasped something that resembled words.

He was not prepared to die. This she knew. He was not going to accept what had been destined. But he had no strength with which to fight death.

Was it really the sow's will that she should save the life of this stranger? She was not certain. Saving a child was not dangerous, she knew. Children were never born evil. Children were like flowers; if they were placed in alien soil early on, they would adjust and blossom. But adults resisted change, for they had difficulty putting down new roots. Perhaps this young man was full of painful memories. Or vengeance. Perhaps he had enormous powers of magic that she, if she saved him, would be responsible for having let loose. It was a great risk to bring him back to life. Perhaps dangerous for her and for everyone at home in the settlement.

Let death choose, she thought. There was no reason to feel ashamed. It was no worse than if she had found a ruined dwelling. One could try to repair it or let nature take its course.

She rose, determined.

The light playing on the icicles hanging from the roof had taken on a deeper shade of blue. Outside, Pitoraq was laying everything waste just as tirelessly as before, and she knew that the rest of the day was his.

Who knew what kind of demons were playing havoc within the stranger?

She would sleep and dream until the storm stilled and she could start on her way home. She would lie in the sow's warm pelt, which was the same golden color as his hair. But his hair was softer.

She must not hesitate any longer, even if death showed no haste in taking him.

Then he sighed deeply.

She turned and looked straight into eyes that were aware and of a deeper blue than the sea. She had never seen anything more beautiful, and she knew at once that she would never forget them.

He held her captive with his eyes, and she let him do so. She saw no trace of evil in his look, only a will just as strong as her own. Of course he was afraid of death and the unknown, that was obvious. But his was not a terror that she need fear. He could not harm her, either. He was too weak for that.

Confused, she saw that he understood what she was thinking, and she felt ashamed.

Her anorak suddenly felt suffocatingly hot. She slowly pulled it over her head, but she knew that his eyes were still fastened on her, his look open and questioning.

"Don't look at me! I don't want to regret what I must do."

But she knew that he saw everything, and she bowed her head and started to groom her hair. That always cleared her thoughts. Besides, it took quite a while to fasten her hair high up on her head, since the knot had to be smooth and tight.

She did not look up, not even while she was taking out the thongs with their beautiful small shells from the pouch in the inner fur. Thongs that held her hair properly but were mainly for decoration. The whole time she felt his eyes, and the sensation of his glance made her hands shake.

If only he would faint again! If only she had gone while he was unconscious. If only she had for once listened to common sense and not let curiosity lead her. Now she could not leave as long as he was awake, for those blue eyes would never cease looking at her. She could not bear their accusation.

Time trickled quietly on. The light waned.

She waited. Nothing changed.

"What would happen if I saved you? You can't manage here alone, can you?" she asked angrily. "I'll become responsible for your life, and I already have enough responsibilities! Do you understand that? I don't even know whether you can survive in the way Human Beings do!"

He could not possibly understand what she was saying. Yet she knew that he understood.

He had no answer and no other hope but her.

She nodded, rose, and walked out of the dwelling.

It was no longer snowing. But Pitoraq was driving enormous storm clouds together in the sky. It might not be possible to leave tomorrow either.

She continued to debate with herself as she opened her bundle.

Part of her cried that it was not too late. She could just refrain from going back in. He would most likely die in the course of the night, and everything would be for him as it had been destined to be. The Great Frost would soon bury the settlement in ice, and the Human Beings could forget their fear of the strangers forever. It sounded sensible. But the other voice spoke more urgently, and she knew that it was not curiosity that led her to cut off a piece of the frozen liver.

He had probably not eaten for many days. Liver was nutritious and easy to swallow for someone who was as weak as he. She would chew the pieces a little first and warm them over the whale-oil lamp. The Old One was supposed to have had the precious liver. But he would surely understand the choice she had made.

He lay exactly as she had left him. His eyes were still open. She realized that he had rallied all his strength in the hope that she would return.

It took ages to feed him a handful of liver morsels. He could scarcely swallow, even though she chewed the tiny bits before she put them in his mouth. Compassionately she watched his exhausted body refusing to be saved. It was only his will that wanted to live. She wondered how long it could last.

She waited patiently while he chewed, vomited, and chewed again. She brought in new snow from outside and filled her mouth with it. Gently she spurted the warm water into his mouth. He slept between each mouthful and every piece, but she massaged his hands until he awakened and kept him conscious until he had swallowed all the food. Not until then did she allow sleep to possess him. Not until then did she allow herself to feel how exhausted she was.

Outside, morning was dawning, and she grew hopeful again. Maybe the sun would rise today.

"Let this be the day that the world turns about!"

But Pitoraq's howling demons were still rushing between the strangers' dwellings, and the sunrise flamed for only a brief moment before the thunder clouds doused it. In the fjord the ice floes lay as tightly packed as before, and the mighty icebergs waited as impatiently as ever to sail.

They have lain still too long, she thought, and suddenly realized how deeply she missed the voices of the icebergs. She longed to hear the thunder when two bergs collided, the loud reports when one of them had to yield, and the rushing sound as the victor slipped out toward the ocean.

The living world had called to her with countless voices. Now the Great Frost had made the world dead and silent.

She could not understand why the Great Frost had come and why it would not release its grip.

The Old One had made more spirit journeys to the Sea's Mother this winter than ever before in his life. Each time he returned to his body in the dwelling where Navarana and the other women and hunters were waiting, he told the same sad story. He had found the Sea's Mother, along with all the game animals, in the blue dwelling on the bottom of the sea. She was very angry, because Her long hair was always filthy and tangled from the sins of Human Beings. She refused to be coaxed into sending Her children back to the coastal hunting grounds, even though the Old Man did his utmost to clean Her hair. Although he swore that everyone would follow Her commandments precisely and always respect nature and the game animals, he knew that the Sea's Mother did not believe the promises. He grew more uneasy with each journey, for even though all those at the settlement did their best to satisfy Her, Her hair was always just as filthy. Simultaneously, the Great Frost continued unrelentingly to devour land and sea. The game did not come, and the Human Beings at the settlement began to lose faith, both in themselves and in their shaman. It was a very perilous situation.

Navarana was the first and only one in a very long time to have any luck hunting. But she was quite aware that it was not due to luck or skill that the sow had been felled. The sow had surrendered itself for the sake of the Human Beings, to prevent their killing one another. Navarana knew what a responsibility had been conferred on her by her luck in hunting. It was a responsibility she could not shirk. Not for anyone.

She had to return home to the settlement as soon as possible with the meat she could manage to carry. She would rest and then start, no matter what the wind and weather. No matter how the stranger was faring. He had survived the night. If his will was only strong enough, he would manage a few days alone. In the event that he was still alive when she came back with the dogsled to get the meat by the beach, she would decide what to do. Maybe it was best to let him remain here, just to give him meat enough for him to manage on his own. The strangers' settlement was his home. Maybe he would rather be alone among all that he was familiar with.

"Fool!" she said sternly. "Would you yourself want to be left in these dismal ruins, left to days full of fear of hungry predators, to nights filled with tormenting ghosts and painful memories? Alone, while you tried to understand what life is all about?"

She snuggled into the bearskin, but the light kept her awake. The golden light that was not in the room but behind her closed eyes. A light that was no longer mute but called to her. The golden light that she could not let slip into the depths of the blue shadows.

Pitoraq had shown her mercy. That she knew as soon as she awoke. The sky was pale white, but the wind had completely calmed. She had not a moment to lose.

While she fed him, she spoke gently and decisively, as if to a child.

"You realize that I have to leave? I can't wait. For I might not get another chance. They're starving at home, can you understand that?"

The blue eyes would not meet hers, and it took a long time before he opened his mouth to eat. It was as if he had withdrawn into himself.

"Just look, I'm really here!"

She showed him her hands.

"Look! I've no horrible sores like your idol on the wall. I only have fine tattoos." She pointed at her chin with its three tattooed lines proving that she was a grown woman.

He ate obediently, but without raising his eyes.

Something was wrong. His will, which had been so strong, was gone. But she could not bother about that now. The most important thing was that he ate a lot before he threw up.

"You'll manage. I know it." She herself could hear that she was lying.

Quickly, she cut the rest of the liver into small pieces and laid them beside his hand. Then she filled a pot with fine snow and placed it by the other hand. She lit the last moss wick and put the blubber in the lamp. There was no more she could do for now.

"I'm coming back, do you hear? I have to, to get the rest of the meat."

He tried to sit up.

Perhaps he wanted to show her that he could manage alone. But his body, which had been a lifeless shell the day before, was suddenly and painfully present. Horrified, she saw his eyes roll back in his head and heard him gasp for air. Spasms of cold shook his body again and again, and large red spots grew on his pale cheeks.

Fever! He now had an even deadlier enemy to fight. She had been busy saving him from starving to death and had not thought about his ice-cold, wet clothes. If she left him like this, he would die the most painful death of all. She could not let it happen. At the very least, he had to have dry, warm clothing.

She hurried out and began to search in the strangers' dwellings.

She found a blanket of heavy cloth, but it was stiff with

ice. There was nothing in the dwellings that could ease his fever.

She cried when she realized that there was only one solution: to wrap him in the sow's golden-white pelt. She struggled with herself for a long time. It was the only thing to do, but the skin was her most precious possession. What would happen to her without its protection? The hide would probably save his life, but did a stranger deserve such a sacrifice? Ashamed, she remembered that it was the Human Beings' greed that bothered the Sea's Mother the most. Navarana acted before she had time to change her mind.

He was awake. His breath came in short gasps. She knew that each breath was like the stabbing of knives. But she was still furious over her sacrifice and would not meet his glance as she spread the beautiful pelt out beside him. Determined, she grasped his quivering arms and drew him up into a sitting position. But when she wanted to drag the wet clothes off him, he struggled against her with all his strength. His rasping breath resembled sobs. He tried to say something, but she was not in the mood to be patient.

"The least you could do is to help me save your life!" she growled. She brutally ripped the heavy garb off him.

She was immediately sorry. Never had she seen anything as defenseless as that naked body. Never had she felt so ruthless. She had revealed his vulnerability, and she would always remember everything about it. That transparent skin where veins ran like blue brooks across the glacier, the skinny chest where the ribs protruded like birds' wings, the abdomen where the blood beat violently, hipbones like naked mountain crags, and his member in that golden underbrush. Shrunken from the shame of being exposed.

Hurriedly she rolled his shivering body over onto the polar-bear skin and covered him. Her cheeks burned as she wrapped him up so that his feet and body were covered and his hands were free. She knew all too well how he felt.

It took time to pack the meat in the strangers' wet blanket. For that, she was grateful. The whole time she heard his teeth chattering from the fever. Probably also from anger, she thought with a prick of conscience as she bound the bundle securely to the smooth poles she would use as sled runners.

She had not meant to humiliate him. She was just angry because she feared the consequences of the choice she had made, because he made her uncertain and confused. Had he been a Human Being, she would have known how to treat him. A Human Being would immediately have understood that she was trying to help, even if she was clumsy. Had he been a Human Being, she would have done the only sensible and natural thing. She would have warmed his body with her own naked body. No Human Being would have felt pitiful and ashamed over being naked.

The stranger had shown himself to be vulnerable in a way that made her feel a moment of intoxicating power. She felt cruel. It was a new and terrifying feeling.

Briskly, she assured herself that he had everything he needed. Still without looking at him.

Then, for the first time, he spoke. Clearly. His voice was hoarse and weak and his language completely incomprehensible. Yet she knew that he was thanking her, and she realized that she sincerely hoped that he might live.

She saw that Pitoraq was still in good humor. He would let the clouds wait to dump their heavy load of snow. The wind was sharp and dry, but it was helpful to have it at her back as she strove up across the slick mountain pass. It was the most dangerous but the quickest way back to the settlement on the promontory.

A long time would pass before she completely grasped what had happened. That nothing would ever again be as it had been destined for her.

SIX

The butterfly in the golden egg. He remembered both the egg and the day quite clearly, even though it was long ago. A day with a summer breeze playing lightly with the waves on the beach and he himself running recklessly across the slick stones and falling. Falling and hitting himself so hard that his crying would not cease.

"I've been saving something really pretty for you, and if you just stop crying, you'll get it," his mother had said. She stood in the waves gathering shells. "Come here, you'll be all right."

He continued to sniff as he limped out into the water. No one could console him as she could.

"Look," she said, putting it in his hand. "An egg from the

sea's foam. Hold it up toward the light and you will see something beautiful."

The piece of amber was large and smooth and milky yellow. He held it up against the sun. "I see only yellow light and something black," he said, disappointed.

"Then you have not looked closely enough." Her laughter was teasing.

"Show me what you see," he begged.

"It won't be something wondrous until you see it for yourself," she answered mysteriously.

She had bent over the shells again, and he knew that she was pleased. She hated seeing him unhappy. Your pain is as my own, she had once said.

What pain she must have suffered when the ironclad men dragged him screaming from her! He had continued to hear the echo of her helpless sobs in his mind long after he had accepted that he would never be able to return home, that he would always belong to the monastery. Did she know that he had the egg with him? The egg with its cloudy surface, which revealed its wonderful secret only after many days' patient polishing: a butterfly in eternal flight, encased within a golden room of stone.

Why had the memory surfaced now? It was strange. He had not thought of it for many years. Now it was continually present in his thoughts, throughout all the feverish days and nights. During the short moments in which he was fully awake and clearheaded, he tried to grasp the memory and decipher it. But it always slid away, and he felt only the loss of something uniquely important.

The violent attacks of fever had given way, and his waking moments slowly grew longer. He concentrated on eating and drinking, quickly, before the pains in his chest overpowered him again. At first the raw liver and meat had made his stomach heave, but soon he experienced only well-being, a sense of strength returning to his body. In his body, which for so long had been only a painful alien shell, he could feel the warm blood flowing through cold arteries. It was a feeling of being born anew, and he thanked God who had sent him deliverance in such a peculiar shape. Then he slept in a golden room with a little butterfly in fluttering flight.

The light awakened him, light winking like a thousand small stars in the ice running from the roof and covering the walls. Light that gave him a wonderful feeling of being free.

He sat up carefully, shaking with fear of the pains. But no knives stabbed his chest. He breathed deeply and with relief. Tentatively, he moved his arms and legs. They were stiff, as if he had slept for months and years. He did not know how long he had been in death's embrace, but death had drawn back. Of that, he was certain.

Gratias agamus Domino Deo nostro!
Lord, hear my voice, for I have called You.
Let Your ears listen attentively to Your servant's prayer.
May Your countenance shine above me, O Lord.
Show me mercy, for I am alone and destitute.
In You, my God, I place all my trust.
O Lord of Mercy, free me from all evil of heart
And let me follow Your commandments.

Never had his prayer been more sincere. Never had he known such gratitude for the gift of life. Life that had been granted to him so that he could withstand all its travail and humbly serve the Lord. Life that he had tried to flee to seek his own celestial bliss.

"Lord, look upon me with mercy . . . *Kyrie eleison . . . Christe eleison . . .*"

His hands folded in prayer were bluish white, almost transparent. Horrified, he saw his chest's sharp bow of ribs, the hollow of his stomach, and the bones of his thighs and calves beneath the loose skin. He was as thin and powerless as an old man. And he was completely naked.

With shame he remembered everything clearly. That fur-covered creature which had leaned over him, which he, in his senseless terror, had exorcised as Satan himself. The creature that had forced him to eat and drink, while he stared disbelievingly into its beautiful black eyes with their flashes of gold. He remembered his terror and bewilderment when that heathen being lifted her arms and he saw a well-formed, golden-brown, female body with firm breasts. He had expected to see a grotesque face with eyes and mouth in the middle of its chest like the monks in Hereford had said the wild heathens beyond the known world had. He had doubted whether he was in possession of his senses, and he wanted her gone and present at the same time.

Suddenly he had known that she felt the same terror of him, the unknown. But she had defied her loathing, the young woman who spoke to him in that oddly musical language. She did everything to save his life, she who tossed her head back proudly when his eyes saw too much.

After this, Brendan had known doubt, strong and nagging. He doubted that it was true that heathens were as soulless as animals. He began to mull over why the Lord had given only humans souls and feelings such as mercy.

He had felt deeply confused by the conflict between what he had newly experienced and the loathing he had learned at the monastery. He knew that, at the very least, she was just as troubled as he.

There had been a moment between them when he felt completely safe. But it was all shattered by the shame of his exposed nakedness.

Desperate, he prayed for enlightenment, but Christ's countenance was dark and silent. He had to find his own answer. He fell asleep, consoled that the ways of the Lord are inscrutable. In His infinite wisdom He had sent an angel of deliverance in a guise of heathen feathers.

The crash of thunder awakened him, and a feeling of not being alone. He opened his eyes wide and felt the blood rushing to his face.

She was standing wreathed in light in the open doorway of the church. At once he understood the meaning of his memory of an egg with a butterfly in golden flight.

SEVEN

It started with a low rumbling, and for a moment Navarana believed that the ice of the fjord was finally breaking up. But when she helped Brendan out into the frost-clear morning, she saw that the ice lay undisturbed. It still resembled gigantic gulls with their wings frozen in flight. Then there was a renewed rumbling, stronger and more threatening, and she heard that it was coming from the mountains above the strangers' settlement. Navarana knew immediately what was about to happen and that they had only a short time to get away.

"Quick!" she said. "You must help me load the sled! Take only what is essential."

He stared at her uncomprehendingly.

"Look!" she screamed, and grabbed his arm. "The inland ice is moving through the cleft! It'll crush everything standing in its way! Don't you understand? Pitoraq has decided to reconquer the land and remove all trace of you strangers!"

Terrified, he saw what she meant.

He had believed that nothing could get worse in this dreadful land. But this, which had built up during the thunderstorms, was much more dangerous than anything he had seen earlier. The pass between the mountains was transformed into a high wall of ice, not a solid wall but a mighty mass of thundering movement.

This was Satan's work. He was certain. It was Satan who wanted to test his strength against God's, and only a divine miracle could save them from being crushed by the masses of ice. Brendan fell to his knees in the snow and started to pray.

"No!" Furious, she pulled him up. "There's no time! We must save the meat on the beach. I can't manage alone."

The husky, wolflike dogs whined like frightened pups as she harnessed them to the sled.

"The dogs know, but you don't understand! How foolish are you, Stranger?"

He did not understand the words, but he understood her rage and terror well enough. All the same he did not obey, for the impossible choice made him powerless. He wanted to save his life, but he could not just flee from Satan, for then he would betray God.

After she had helped him back to life, he had decided that he would begin God's work at the Northmen's abandoned farm. Here, where so many of the brothers had lost their lives, he would atone for his sins and do penance. He would be alone, perhaps for the rest of his life on earth, but that did not bother him. A great many of God's servants had lived a solitary life. Saint Augustine, too, had chosen the chastening solitude of the desert. It had not occurred to Brendan that he would be forced to leave God's last bulwark in this heathen land. But now he suddenly realized that he must either die without having atoned for his sin or flee from his vow to God.

"Lord, guide me!"

The redeemed soul is God's dwelling.

He was not certain whether he had heard it or it was the solace of his own thoughts.

"Decide! I can't wait any longer!" Her voice was sharp with terror.

He hesitated no longer. But he could not abandon the crucifix. He ran into the church.

She was staring, flabbergasted and furious, when he came out again.

"Don't you understand anything? You can't take that heavy idol of yours with you! The dogs must have strength enough to pull the meat home."

But he had already given up too much. He could not give in on this, even if it meant that she left him behind.

He stood there, silent and inflexible. The great wooden figure was hanging in his arms like a sorrowful child.

It was incomprehensible that he was being so stubborn. Like a lemming, she thought. Of all the creatures of the Sea's Mother it was only the lemming that did not have the sense to accept the demands of nature. Only it would plunge meaninglessly to its death. But, like the lemming, he was brave, and reluctantly she had to admire him for it.

The rumbling from the mountains grew to a violent roar, and she knew that Pitoraq's patience had reached its breaking point. The great inland ice was on the move, and it was not to be stopped.

Quickly, she grabbed the wooden figure and bound it to the sled. Then, she tossed him the hunting garb that the Old One had let her borrow. She saw that the *kamiks*, trousers, and anorak were quite small. But if he traveled in his long outfit and those thin, short boots of his, he would either be badly frostbitten or freeze to death. That would mean more bother for her and loss of time. She could not risk that now.

"You'll get your way, but you're going to dress yourself like a Human Being!" she snarled. Irritated, she saw that he was smiling with relief.

"Dress sensibly, or you'll freeze your manhood off." She pointed spitefully. "But maybe that would be best; then there would never be more strangers in the Land of Human Beings!"

She might as well have slapped his face.

His blue eyes flashed as he grabbed the clothes and turned away. Quickly, he pulled on the trousers and *kamiks*, tore off his habit, and put on the anorak. Finally, he pulled on his heavy garb and turned toward her. His mouth was a thin line when he began to speak. It was not difficult to understand that he had had enough of humiliation.

They did not exchange glances as they fought to hold the sled on course down across the slope to the fjord. He followed alertly all that she did and helped as best he could when her strength failed. She knew that he was still weak and that he had to learn everything. But never would he give her the chance to treat him like a child again.

In silence they dug out the meat and tied it securely to the sled. They worked closely and in rhythm. It was as if

they had never done anything else. But the distance between them was great. Distance created by the same sort of
stubbornness and the same disquieting feeling of always
having known of each other.

They dared not rest before they were safe on the crest of
the ridge, far from the settlement. Exhausted from tension
and the trip, they lay down in the snow and watched the
ultimate attack of the ice. The howling of the dogs was
drowned by the roaring of masses of ice plunging out from
the cleft and surging across the settlement. The sky was
covered by a cloud of crushed ice. The deafening attack
lasted for a long, long time. Then, it became utterly silent,
and they saw only a white sea stretching tranquilly out to
the ice in the fjord. Not a dwelling was visible any longer.
Every trace was wiped out.

Not until then did they look at each other, and both
knew what the other was thinking:

I would not have made it without you.

Fortunately, no words were to be found for such feelings.

Navarana carefully assessed whether they ought to make
camp on the crest of the ridge. There were still many hours
left before it grew completely dark. With luck she could
reach home. But she would have to drive the dogs ex-

tremely hard, maybe beyond the bounds of what they could stand. She had seen all too many dogs lying dead from exhaustion in the sled's tracks when their owners had driven them too hard. She had bred and trained this pack of proud, half-wild dogs herself. She knew they would follow her blindly. To death itself if she so decided. Neither she nor the dogs were well acquainted with the rugged terrain along the fjord, and never before had her dogs pulled so heavy a load. Even small obstacles could mean delays. If darkness surprised them, both they and the dogs would be badly off.

Brendan had never seen anything like it. She squatted among the dogs, and he could have sworn that they were whispering to one another. She gentle and singing, those huge beasts, reminiscent of the frightening wolfhounds of his childhood, whining devotedly and listening with tilted heads. There was an intimacy between them that he had seen only between people who loved each other deeply, and he was certain that the dogs would race to the ends of the earth for her.

What he saw made his doubt grow even stronger. It was not true that animals and heathens did not possess noble feelings. For the first time he began to speculate over why he had been told such lies. Was it because the Church's learned men did not know better? Or did they purposely lie? In any case, it could not be God's intent that his servants should disdain heathens and force them into submission.

God was not so unjust. Not *his* God, the Father who had created the world and every living thing in it with such love.

Eventually, Navarana rose and glanced shyly at him. Then she got her knife and began slashing the hard snow into perfect square blocks. She worked quickly and without stopping, and he stood by uncertainly, watching the number of blocks grow.

"Show me what to do," he asked meekly.

She nodded, smiling at him for the very first time.

He felt warmth flashing through his body.

Carefully, he followed her directions: first, blocks in a circle, then block on block for a dome-shaped house of snow. When they were finished, the sky was overcast with blue-black clouds and the wind cut their flesh.

"Feed the dogs!" she shouted.

But he did not dare. For he knew that they disliked him just as intensely as they loved her.

"Well then, carry the meat in. Don't forget your idol, or it will be chewed to splinters by morning!"

She laughed, and it was the teasing laughter of his mother. There was nothing about this wildcat that reminded him of his dependable, thoughtful mother. But they both had the same power. That mysterious power which had made him feel that he was shut out of his mother's life. He had never known other women than his mother. Never been alone with a girl his own age. Suddenly he became aware of his helplessness. He knew that it would only grow worse.

Navarana lay awake for a long time, listening to his uneasy breathing. He had to be boiling in all those clothes. But he had refused to do as any sensible Human Being would, disrobe to his bare skin as soon as the whale-oil lamp started giving off warmth. Perhaps he could not believe that the igloo stored warmth. Perhaps he was just afraid of being naked around her. She had not tried to force him. She had humiliated him often enough, she thought with shame. It bothered her that she had treated him as she had. Was it because she had never before met a man so awkward and ignorant, so completely unable to manage even the most ordinary things?

Or was she trying to frighten him away?

The Old One had looked at her for a long time as she told how she had found the stranger and why she had saved him.

"He has hair the same color as the sow's coat."

"Do you know which path you have chosen?" he said quietly.

"I've not chosen anything at all. I just saved his life," she said abruptly. Though she knew that she did not need to defend herself, she continued anyway: "I only did my duty as a Human Being. I thought you would appreciate that."

"Don't be angry, Navarana, for then you will just be deaf to opinions other than your own." The Old One was solemn.

"You've saved a life *and* you've set something in motion. Something you alone can't control. You've no idea where this will lead you."

She wanted to say that it was not as he believed and that she was grown up enough to manage for herself. But she pressed her lips together tightly.

"Be careful, my child. You can very easily lose your way in your own life."

He had not said more. And she, who always listened carefully to the Old One, had turned a deaf ear to him.

As she stared into the little yellow flame of the lamp, she thought uneasily of the Old One. He was the master. She was the pupil. He was common sense and she was curiosity. He had quite often said that she should not just blindly obey him but think for herself and make her own choices. He had not directly said that she should use both her common sense and her curiosity. And should not let herself be steered by the one or the other. Now she knew it had not been common sense that had led her into taking the stranger along with her. She had no idea what her decision would lead to, for him or for her.

EIGHT

It was late twilight when they reached the top of the last low mountain ridge and saw the settlement in the valley below. The valley had the shape of a whale-oil lamp. The low mountains protected the settlement against wind and wild storms. The dwellings of the Human Beings, which lay facing the fjord and the previously plentiful hunting and fishing grounds, were now the only flickering flame of life in the valley.

Relieved, she saw that smoke was still rising from each and every one of the round, snow-covered dwellings. Lazy white smoke spiraling toward the thunder-blackened sky.

It was an illusion, Navarana knew. The smoke was not lazy. There was just too little fuel left. She could scarcely remember the last time they had harvested withy, peat, and heather from the valley's bounty. Or how long it had been since they had helped themselves from the piles of sun-baked driftwood on the shore. The expeditions for fuel were long now and just as demanding as the hunt for fresh food. All too often both the fuel gatherers and the hunters came back empty-handed.

The settlement was precisely as it had been when she left it. She knew that in the dwellings the adults were sleeping a sleep that resembled the hibernation of animals. In that long dream a person felt neither hunger nor privation nor terror of the future. Human Beings had always used the long sleep to help them through catastrophes. But that trancelike condition was dangerous, for one did not notice death superceding the dream.

She saw the slumbering dwellings and felt the same desperation that had driven her out to hunt the polar bear. At the time she had said that it made no sense for Human Beings not to struggle for their own survival, but the adults had looked at her as if she were an ignorant child. Only the Old One understood. He was grateful that she would dare to risk all so that the world would turn.

"Take care of my sisters," she had said to the Foster Mother. And she knew that while the other adults dreamt of better times, the Foster Mother and the Old One would be awake and see to it that all the families' children got something to eat from the little there was.

Now she saw that the children were out playing as usual. They were playing ball and tumbling around in the snow with the pups that had not yet become food. Those that were still being saved for new sled teams. She heard her two little sisters howling in rivalry with the pups, as they ran on the ice down to the shore in the quickly failing light. The Foster Mother came out and called the sisters in to bed, and Navarana saw them scrabble obediently up across the slope and disappear into the dwelling. With a pang of conscience she thought that they were well-off. As well-off as children could be who did not yet know that death-by-starvation was stalking its prey at the settlement.

The sled dogs whined, impatient to get down to the settlement for food and rest. She shushed them. She wanted to wait as long as possible, until the settlement was at rest for the night. Then she could come down almost unnoticed.

The dogs lay still, muzzles between their paws, and glanced at her, ready to rush off if she gave the slightest sign.

She had driven them hard, and it had been a terribly strenuous journey. Everything had gone so very much slower than both she and the dogs were accustomed to. All because of Brendan, the stranger. The ignorant, clumsy, and contentious Brendan who now lay sleeping on the sled as if unconscious.

Brendan. She tasted the word with its foreign sounds. Their names were the only things they had tried to teach each other.

She had put knowing his name to good use, since she had shouted it often enough during the long journey by sled. Sometimes angrily, because he would not listen. Sometimes warningly, when he did not understand the dangers, and finally, sympathetically, when he was so exhausted that his legs refused to support him.

There was nothing he knew how to do, not even how to move about in snow. Time and again she and the dogs had waited as he floundered and fell, floundered and fell again. But he always got to his feet, stubborn as ever. And however much she begged or scolded, he still refused to remove that long garment, which was stiff with ice and caused him to trip even more often.

She became so furious that she wanted to scream, and yet she could not help admiring his courage. Alienated and forsaken by his own kind, he was like a newborn babe in the Human Beings' Land. But he stood his ground with pride and without the least complaint.

What kind of reception would he get? Before, when all

was normal and the seasons changed as they should, people would have been slightly reserved toward a stranger like him. But he would have received food and shelter just the same, for no one was as hospitable and generous as the Human Beings at the settlement when there was anything to be shared.

Now she was not certain how they would receive Brendan, the stranger, or what they would say to her who had brought him along. She who was an outsider herself.

It was best for the Old One to meet Brendan first. She knew that his opinion greatly influenced the opinions of everyone else.

The Old One's dwelling lay a little apart from the cluster of other dwellings. There he lived alone.

A shaman must be undisturbed by the clamor of daily life, he said. Everyone respected the shaman's need to have peace to fly between all the worlds and time to interpret the often mysterious messages he received on his spirit journeys.

Navarana knew how deeply he disliked the quarreling between men and women, which was steadily growing worse. Women who accused the men of being lazy and poor hunters, men who accused the women of having ruined the hunters' luck by not observing the Sea's Mother's taboos strictly enough.

"Quarreling will surely not bring the game back!" grumbled the Old One, and withdrew into his dwelling.

Navarana had dared to follow after him uninvited.

In the beginning he had treated her like a stray dog. She had graciously been allowed to sit by the lamp. He had shared some bits of dried meat and blubber with her; then he had brusquely asked her to go. But even though she felt his strong dislike, she returned, and he slowly began to take an interest in her.

"What do you want?" he had asked dismissively.

"To learn," Navarana had answered instantly.

She had waited ages for him to ask.

"To learn what, may I ask?"

The Old One was tired of trying to teach people who merely quarreled.

"To learn to fly, like you," she had answered bravely.

"Neither you nor I will live that long!" He laughed, but he realized that the young girl was serious.

She never mentioned it again, and he did not ask.

She continued to come and sit quietly by the lamp, and he began to wonder whether she perhaps possessed a shaman's powers. He never said so out loud, but he began to tell her the story of the Ancestors.

"Once upon a time the world was one land from east to west, from north to south, and all Human Beings were one family. In time, land and Human Beings became divided, and everything was different. But as you know, the time before ours does not die. It can be buried or be repressed, but it always lives on somewhere in us and behind us, and we can always find it again in the songs and tales of the Ancestors. Therefore we guard the songs of the Ancestors with our very lives."

She was happy that he had been willing to open up the world to her.

He was happy to have an attentive listener, perhaps also an apprentice who could be educated as a new keeper of the Ancestors' treasures.

Navarana got up. It was time to meet the Old One.

The dogs were on their feet immediately.

She whispered to them, and they set off without a whimper.

Brendan quickly rose. Not for anything in the world would he give her reason to call him again, impatiently, angrily, or—worst—sympathetically. He did not need her pity; he knew all too well that he had her to thank for his very existence. He had never been indebted to anyone before. It had always been the others who were indebted to him. It had been that way ever since he started as an errand boy and later as a novice in the monastery in England. Untiringly, he had cared for the old monks and the plague-stricken poor; he had helped women away from the place of execution when their husbands were put to death, and he had consoled the orphans. The quiet triumph of being the giver, one who was merciful and unselfishly serving the Lord, had been payment enough. Never had he thought about what it felt like to be dependent on another person. Far less to live at the mercy of a stranger. But now he knew, and he hated every single reminder that he could not manage on his own.

"Pride is the worst of sins," he mumbled between clenched teeth, while his head boiled with agitated emotions.

The long trip by sled, filled with surprises and dangers he could not even have dreamed of, was one that Navarana had had to manage alone. His contribution had been to delay her and the dogs. He was certain that if the dogs could have spoken, they would have asked her to leave him lying behind in the snow.

The continual humiliations made him befuddled with tiredness. He did not notice where the sled was going and was scarcely awake when it stopped. He was happy that she had stopped on the mountain ridge. But when she stirred, he was quickly by her side, as if to say that he was managing for himself and ready to help her.

She did not notice him.

"That's where I live." Navarana pointed.

Brendan saw the smoke from the small domed houses. It was a relief to see how few houses there were. There could not be many heathens living there, and they were perhaps just as harmless as she. In any case, his fate lay in God's hands.

He nodded and tried to smile at her.

She showed him how to keep the sled on course as she traversed the long slope.

It was a nearly soundless trip, but outside the dwellings the pups, lying with their muzzles buried in their warm tails, caught scent of the sled dogs and soon started a whining and howling that awakened the whole settlement.

"Navarana! Navarana! What have you got there?"

It was the Foster Father shouting.

"I have enough meat for everyone!" she answered. "Just wait until I have stopped by the Old One's."

Quickly, she maneuvered the foreign idol off and shoved Brendan, with the idol in his arms, through the entryway of the Old One's dwelling.

He rose from his bunk.

The lamp was lit and shone with a steady flame.

"I've been waiting," he merely said. "Leave me alone with the stranger while you calm the curious with meat."

He invited the stranger to sit close by the lamp.

Everything grew quiet as they stared at each other.

Brendan saw a man whose body was entirely withered with age and whose face and hands were gnarled and burned black by wind and weather. But his eyes were as young and clear as the night sky, and just as unfathomable. Brendan was not sure what he had been expecting, but certainly not this. Not a man with the same authority that he had encountered among teachers at the monastery. The old heathen's glance resembled that of Brother Gareth. Distant yet penetrating. He was completely unprepared for the feeling that the old man was reading his innermost thoughts, and he lowered his eyes to protect himself.

The old man chuckled, and Brendan felt even more transparent. There was nothing he could do to prevent this heathen with the long gray hair from reading him like an open book. It was an unpleasant feeling.

He clasped the large cross to his breast and said the Paternoster several times.

The old heathen continued to stare. There was great amusement deep within his eyes. It could burst forth in laughter at any moment. Brendan would then feel totally compromised.

"*Ave Maria*, Hail Mary . . . *gratia plena*, full of grace . . . *Dominus tecum*."

He took out the little icon of the mourning Virgin Mary and the sainted John on either side of Jesus Christ on the cross, which he always wore at his breast. He kissed it long and fervently. He had received this sacred icon after his pilgrimage to Canterbury, as proof that he had prayed at the grave of the martyr Saint Thomas. It was his most precious possession, and he always wore it along with the relic Brother Gareth had given him before his journey to Greenland. The relic was a joint from the holy Saint Brendan's thumb, which Brother Gareth himself had worn for many years. Brendan would not accept it, but Brother Gareth was determined: "You shall have this holy bone from the body of your great namesake as thanks for your unselfish deed. It will protect and keep you from all dangers and temptations."

More than once Brendan had been grateful that he had accepted it. That little knuckle had given him the strength to endure many trials. When he held it in his hand, he thought he could detect the scent of honeysuckle and lavender, precisely that paradisical scent that the holy Saint Brendan himself had experienced on his journey. Now Brendan needed the strength to withstand a trial that was vastly different from the trials his holy namesake had endured.

The silence and heat were oppressive. He felt heavy and sleepy yet light and dizzy. He wanted to sleep, but his mind fluttered alertly around his terror of the old man's peculiar power. He wanted to flee, but there was no place to hide.

Then the old man moved. With a commanding look, he stretched out both hands.

Reluctantly, Brendan laid the cross in his arms.

The Old One meticulously studied this figure of Jesus Christ, outstretched and suffering, before giving it back. Then he bade Brendan to remove his clothes. Brendan hesitated, but he knew that he would soon acquiesce.

The Old One also took his time looking over the monk's robe, the rosary, and the little cross of silver. Brendan noticed that, even though the old man's face was expressionless, he treated everything with great respect, sitting thoughtfully for a long time with the relic and the tiny crucifix in his hands. And quite suddenly Brendan realized that he himself was studying the old man, was trying to find out what thoughts were stirring behind the heathen's impassive expression.

"Our Lord Jesus Christ," said Brendan softly, pointing at the icon of calvary. "God's only begotten Son, who died for mankind's sins. That is His Holy Mother, Mary, standing by His side. She is grieving over her crucified son."

Gently, the Old One gave all the objects back to him.

Then, for a time, he stared ponderingly into Brendan's eyes before he turned his glance toward the flame in the whale-oil lamp.

Respect, thought Brendan. He is showing me respect!
For the first time in a long while Brendan felt joy.

When Navarana came in, she looked tensely from the one silent man to the other.

"You've made a remarkable discovery," said the Old One. "I'm not certain that it was wise of you to have brought the stranger here. Only time will tell," he hastily added.

"Tell me what you see," she begged.

"This is no evil or murderous stranger. I've seen him naked. He has no weapon. He has no killing in mind either. But he has plenty of rage and pride. You've surely already noticed that, I would imagine?"

Navarana flushed.

"What do you mean, a remarkable discovery?" she quickly asked.

"The charms are extremely important to him," continued the Old One without answering her. He disliked her trying to hurry the story along.

"His love of the spirits must be very great, greater than a son's love of his father and mother."

"Are they strong charms? Dangerous?" Navarana had feared they were ever since she first saw the white, bleeding wooden figure.

"They probably have a very strong power for him, but they're not dangerous to us. Yet we know nothing about who his spirits are or what the charms are meant to aid him with. In any case it can't be hunting or fishing."

He did not mention the tiny relic that the stranger wore alongside the cross at his breast, a desiccated knuckle bone that without doubt had come from a man. Navarana had apparently not seen that ominous relic, and he saw no reason to frighten her unnecessarily. The stranger was no cannibal, of that he was convinced. The bone probably had magic power for the stranger, but it had lain dry and cold in his own hand.

"Now, it's important that you and I let everyone at the settlement know that he and his charms can't harm us," the Old One continued. "It'll be difficult enough for them to accept one more mouth to feed, let alone one of the colorless strangers."

"But I'm the one who brought the food," she said hotly.

"Yes, but you surely aren't forgetting that you and your little sisters are indebted to this settlement that is so severely stricken with hunger?" he answered sharply.

She fell silent. It was quiet for some time.

"The remarkable thing is," said the Old One after a while, "that the stranger is filled with a longing so burning that I've seldom seen its like. I've met many who sought to become shamans, also from lineages that were not of the Human Beings. But never before have I met anyone so absorbed by, almost desperate with, longing. As if he has lost direction."

The Old One looked questioningly at her.

She remembered Brendan's despair when he had to abandon the strangers' doomed settlement.

She nodded.

"Look for yourself." The Old One waved a hand toward Brendan. He was sitting unmoving, staring past the flame and into himself.

"You've found a stranger who might have lost his direction but will never stop seeking his spirits. And you've bound yourself to his fate."

Navarana wanted to protest, but she let it go. He knew what she herself would not admit, what had made her wait so long to come down to the settlement. She had feared that the Old One would say that the stranger was a danger—to everyone at the settlement. For she now knew that she could not have sent him away, could never have condemned him to fight against the Severe Winter all alone. Never.

NINE

"You can't teach old dogs new tricks."

The Old One had repeated it again and again.

She still had difficulty believing that no one at the settlement would accept Brendan's being there, even if he was not a burden to anyone. No one said anything, either to Navarana or to him. No one did anything, but they all tried to avoid him, as if he were cursed or suffering from a dangerous illness. Even her little sisters, who otherwise followed her everywhere, started to run when they saw him. After a while they stopped coming when she called them.

Brendan, for his part, became steadily more shy and reticent, and Navarana knew that he was suffering from their fear.

"What's the matter?"

Navarana seated herself in front of the Old One and looked him straight in the eye. She no longer asked politely for an explanation.

He sat silent for a long time.

"Guilt," he sighed finally.

"Guilt?"

"Old feelings of guilt."

Then he told about the relationship between the strangers and the Human Beings. Long ago they had lived peaceably side by side. They had traded and helped one another, even in the battle against the murderous strangers who were not of the same lineage. All went well until a quarrelsome woman named Navaranaaq became bored and told everyone willing to listen at the settlement that the strangers planned to attack and kill the Human Beings. Then she went to the strangers and said the Human Beings planned to attack and kill the strangers, and so she continued to spread her stories until the minds of all were poisoned with suspicion. At the settlement the men decided to gain an advantage over the strangers, and one day when the strangers' men were out hunting, the Human Beings attacked the strangers' settlement and killed the women and children. When the strangers' men returned, they took a terrible revenge. They would have wiped one another out if the Human Beings had not regained their senses and understood that it was Navaranaaq who was behind it all. They punished her with a cruel and painful death, but no punishment could bring back the dead and no remorse could restore trust between the two peoples.

"Such is the truth, and it's terrible," the Old One concluded. "Of course, it means nothing that you are the evil woman's namesake."

"My name was whispered in my ear at birth. I carry the name of my great-grandmother," said Navarana hotly. "She was a great and good woman, and her soul lives on in me."

"Precisely. And one day you'll be like her." The Old One smiled.

"Do you believe that?"

"I know," he answered mysteriously. "But you probably won't become so here."

Navarana brooded over what he had told her. It made it easier to understand why they were all keeping their distance, but it was becoming steadily more difficult to grasp how Brendan or she herself could continue to be at the settlement.

"It feels like waiting for a great thunderstorm," she said to the Old One.

"I'm glad that you have seen that for yourself," he answered. "Then you must also understand what we must do."

"We?"

"Yes, we. You know that you can't continue living here. You'll have to travel far to find a new settlement. You can't manage it alone. You don't have enough experience. Brendan doesn't have enough strength. Besides, he must learn to live as a Human Being. Luckily, young dogs can learn new tricks." He smiled. "And I have great experience with dogs."

"But these are your relations; it's here you belong," she protested.

"I belong everywhere, as you well know. And my relations will benefit from being forced to act on their own. As long as I'm here, they'll continue to depend on my ability to mollify the Sea's Mother for them. It's time they themselves strove to win back their luck at hunting. But you ought to convince your little sisters to stay. They're doing well here, and our journey may be very long and strenuous."

Navarana went to her foster parents and had a long talk with them. They were clearly relieved when she said that she would leave the settlement with Brendan and go out to the coast, then north and westward toward the settlement of her father's family. The Foster Mother immediately offered to care for Navarana's sisters, and Navarana was extremely happy that she was spared from having to ask on their behalf. But to her sisters she could not bear to say anything yet. And she left it to the Old One himself to tell everyone that he was leaving.

It was easier to be at the settlement after that. The storm that everyone had feared had immediately blown over. Now it only remained for them to wait until nature's violent storms had stilled. Sooner or later Pitoraq would tire of his wild ride across the sky, and they could set out for the coast.

The Old One used the waiting period well, and Brendan's transformation was soon apparent to everyone. It was like seeing a chrysalis become a butterfly, thought Navarana. He had voluntarily put aside his garment when the Old One started to teach him to use the spear and harpoon. He practiced with persistence and shone with satisfaction when he hit the target. She even heard him laughing and singing.

Then the Old One came to her and said, "You must sew *kamiks* for Brendan from your polar-bear skin. Sew high ones like the women in the north do."

"I won't!" she exclaimed.

"You can't allow him to travel in the clothing he was able to borrow from me. The trousers are all too short. You know quite well that he'll freeze if he doesn't have higher boots. What will you do then?"

She kept silent, feeling tears of anger stinging her eyes.

"Your sow gave her life for your sake. Shouldn't you be generous to him? Otherwise, it's difficult to understand why you've done so much to save his life."

He turned on his heel and left, and he did not speak to her until she brought out the skin and began to cut.

While she was sewing, she was with her sisters as often as they wished. She told them about their family in the north, about the great polar-bear hunter that was their father, about the beautiful throat singer that was their mother; she could sing like the wind across the ice and whistle exactly like the snow sparrow. When the sisters went to sleep, she lay down between them and, whispering, told about her wonderful polar-bear hunt and the sow's great power, and it slowly dawned on them that she was going to leave them. Just as slowly she realized that she could not stand losing them.

She lay awake each evening, thinking of her father and mother and of herself and her sisters, who had only one another.

She noticed that the Old One's lamp was always shining.

And she heard mumbling voices, and sometimes laughter, as from those who are thriving on teaching, and learning from, each other.

Brendan had never experienced such joy. It was as if he were thirsty and could not get enough to drink. The Old One gladly ladled up from his spring of knowledge, and there never seemed to be an end to his patience. Brendan had had many teachers as he was growing up in the monastery, but never anyone whom he had learned so much from so quickly. Each day that passed he became more certain that he would be able to manage. He could handle both spear and harpoon; he could repair tools and knew how a sled should be steered.

It was just language that was difficult for them, and it took time before Brendan understood what was wrong. He picked up the Old One's soft Greenlandic easily enough, but the Old One was not satisfied just to teach, he wanted to understand Brendan's language, too. But all Brendan's attempts to teach him Latin failed. Not because the Old One could not learn but because the language of the Holy Church suddenly felt stiff on Brendan's tongue. And he could not imagine how he would explain what his prayers meant without his simultaneously preaching God's tenets. Brendan mulled it over. He yearned to carry out God's will and convert the Old One, but it did not feel right to begin now. He himself was a pupil, and he knew too little about the Old One's belief for his own preaching to be convincing.

The Old One stared at him. Then he said quietly, "Is it actually the language of your heart that you're trying to teach me?"

"What do you mean?"

"Is this the language you learned from your mother?"

"No," said Brendan. "Not at all! My mother's language was Celtic. It's beautiful and musical, though different from yours, but it rolls off the tongue just as naturally."

"Tell me about your mother," said the Old One.

And for the first time Brendan told another person about the wound that would never heal, about his mother with her boundless patience and warm laughter, about Ireland's green meadows and fragrant sea breeze. Not until long afterward did he realize that he had described the Garden of Eden.

"The sled is too heavily loaded," she said harshly.

They were ready to leave.

"What's the matter?" asked Brendan.

He had put on the *kamiks* of polar-bear skin and was wearing them with obvious pride.

"It's too heavy."

She pointed to the large cross that he had wrapped in an old sealskin.

He grew pale. "I can't leave it." He looked imploringly at her.

Tight-lipped, she stared at the bundle without answering. Her two little sisters pressed themselves close against her and did not release her from their gaze.

The Old One saw it all and knew what was going on.

"What do you want?"

"I can't leave them behind," she whispered. "But his piece of wood has taken up their place on the sled."

"Are you certain that they're not safer here?"

"That may be, but we need one another."

The Old One saw in her sisters' eyes that it was true.

A sacrifice for a sacrifice, thought he, and walked slowly over to the sled.

The other hunters and women flocked behind him in curiosity.

The Old One drew the sealskin off the cross and lifted the cross high in the air.

"Your idol is pretty heavy," he said aloud.

Behind him there was the sound of frightened gasps. No one had seen the stranger's idol, which had lain hidden in the Old One's dwelling.

"You'll be doing us all a favor, if you leave your idol behind," he continued with convincing authority.

"That's my Holy Father's Son," began Brendan.

"But you have him within yourself and by your heart."

The Old One pointed to the two small girls. "You must sacrifice the idol for their sakes."

His voice brooked no contradiction, and Brendan knew that he once again was faced with a completely impossible choice. He sank to his knees and kissed the feet of Jesus, while he prayed fervently for forgiveness.

Everyone waited respectfully, motionless.

The Old One stared silently at Navarana.

"Why did you do that in such a mean way?" She saw in his eyes.

She stared resolutely back.

"Always remember that everything is double," said the Old One aloud. "The sun and moon, sea and sky, life and death, animal and Human Being and their souls; everything is double within the same whole. Also hatred and love. Never forget that."

Never before had he spoken to her this way, as if she were a difficult child. She felt her face burning with shame, and she wished fervently that she could undo her hateful deed. It was true that the sled would be too heavy with both his idol and her sisters. It was sensible to leave it behind. But it was the way in which she had done it. She had wanted to experience that dizzying feeling of triumph when she once again showed herself to be superior.

She turned quickly to beg forgiveness.

But his eyes were as cold as the glacier, and his voice hard with disdain when he said, "I well understand that you do not want to leave without your sisters. But must you treat my faith so hatefully? I thought you had a soul, Heathen, and that you could feel love like a human. Now I see that I have made a mistake. May God be merciful to you."

She stiffened, and all shame disappeared, as if blown away by the wind. Stubbornly her eyes met his, and she and he remained standing like that with their eyes locked in anger, while the Old One quietly carried the cross into the dwelling of the oldest hunter.

"This will be a difficult journey," he merely said.

The men and women around him mumbled sympathetically.

"I expect you to spare Brendan's idol as long as possible," he continued. "But I also know how bitterly you need dry, fine wood like this. If his spirits are of the right sort, you will be forgiven. Nevertheless, do not forget to thank his spirit and the Sea's Mother for the gift."

It was a dry, cold morning. The first in ages that promised to be windless. Navarana tucked the little girls in well. They soon lay down on the sled to sleep. The Old One stood on the back of the sled, and Navarana and Brendan ran on either side of it. There are more than two worlds between them, thought the Old One. He wondered when they would see that they were two parts of a whole.

TEN

Brendan saw three black dots against the enormous whiteness that was either land or sea or sky. He was not certain, for all the forms, outlines, and shadows in the landscape were erased, and the sky and horizon had fused into a limitless white wall, which they slowly approached. The wall could be three hundred yards ahead of them or terribly far away. Perhaps it was not there at all. It was impossible to know, for even though he strained to find fixed points for judging distances, he was always mistaken. The lack of direction and distance was confusing and after a while made him desperate. He had long since lost a sense of time. Without any sense of their surroundings, it was as if they walked and walked without moving. Hour after hour, day after day, in white space.

Brendan had heard the Northmen's accounts of the "white hell." Dazzling whiteness that blinded people and created illusory distances that drove them out of their minds. But he had paid no more attention to those stories than to the other frightening stories told about this merciless land.

On the whole, thought Brendan bitterly, there was very little he had paid attention to, whether people, land, or animals, in all the time he had been on Greenland. He had been too absorbed in himself. He had tried to fulfill Pope Nicholas's command. But the few poor souls who had not fled from the deadly winter had need of nothing more than his thoughtful care and the last rites. In most of the small parishes the Holy Church was deserted, just as the farms were. Brendan had not pondered why the once-flowering parishes now lay desolate. He had been satisfied to live his harsh life at the lonely farm lying farthest up the fjord. With the brothers he had lived in the same way as in the monastery at home. But he had happily undertaken all the exhausting trips to seek out errant souls. For all that he had renounced and undergone brought him closer to the fulfillment of his dream of a vision journey and eternal peace.

Unfortunately, Navarana was right. He was as ignorant as a child. And he had only himself to thank for it. For if he had only been aware of nature and people's lives, and not just been interested in the salvation of their souls, he would perhaps now know how he himself was to survive. Then he would not have had to fumble blindly, exhausted by stumbling over blocks of ice that he thought were a flat field or falling in holes that he could not see.

For a time after they had left the settlement, he had trotted beside the sled. Anger had given him unsuspected strength, and he did not want to provide Navarana the pleasure of having to help him. Covertly he studied Navarana and the Old One, saw how they ran at a moderate tempo behind or beside the sled, then threw themselves on it in a half-sitting position going downhill, while holding it on a steady course with one leg, only to slide off and support the sled going uphill. It looked simple, but they had the sled's movements and the dogs' rhythm in their bodies, and their feet read the lay of the land through the soft soles of their *kamiks*.

His body knew nothing about all this, and it protested against the unfamiliar.

"You should follow behind, in the sled tracks. There you'll be of most use," said the Old One. He could have added that Brendan quite unnecessarily used up all his strength making a track beside the sled, but he would not be impolite. He was worried about the young man. The old man could well understand the rage driving him, for Navarana had shown a petty vindictiveness that was completely incomprehensible. It was also dangerous for her. The Old One, given the opportunity, wanted to speak seriously with her. But this was not really the time. Now all that mattered was for them to get where they were going as quickly as possible. Where there was perhaps still hope to be found. Where Navarana's two sisters could be completely safe.

He would just have to travel with two hurricanes.

He didn't worry about Navarana. She was concentrating on maneuvering the fully laden sled in that rugged terrain along the fjord. It was worse for Brendan. His strength would soon be at an end. He could die from exhaustion, like an overeager sled dog.

Brendan was grateful for the Old One's advice.

It was a lot easier to run in the sled tracks, and the sled's movements warned him in time to avoid falling. He focused his willpower on keeping an even pace, and he soon felt that his muscles hurt less with that rocking rhythm, and his rage slowly ebbed away.

They had traveled for many days when Brendan saw the three black dots. At first they were almost invisible and motionless against all the whiteness; then, it seemed obvious that they were coming nearer. It was the first sign of life since they had left the settlement. They had traveled past the ice-covered farms of the Northmen and spent the night at deserted settlements. The Old One had become more and more grim at each empty sod house and each rack that was without kayaks, and he mumbled to Navarana: "I am glad that we took your little sisters along. Now I just hope that the others at the settlement will soon come to their senses and follow the game."

Brendan wanted to be quite certain before he warned the Old One and Navarana about what he had seen. They were busy maneuvering the sled down an extremely steep slope. It was difficult, and they were obviously exhausted. The dogs were not of much help. They were worn out from having run for two days without food. Their tails, usually curled in high spirits, were hanging limp, and they were snapping angrily at one another.

Brendan knew how important it was if he was right. It could mean the difference between life and death. He strained his eyes to see clearly, staring until the tears stung. He was certain that the dots were steadily coming closer, floating slowly. But they were not black as he at first thought. They were as red as blood.

"I see something living!" He shouted. "Something is moving, far out there, three blood-red dots."

He turned, elated, toward them, and Navarana saw that his eyes, those clear, sky-blue eyes, were glassy and completely covered by a web of blood vessels.

The Old One grabbed him by the arms and turned him quickly away from the almost invisible disk of the sun.

"What do you see now," he said.

"I see . . . a terrible red mist . . . ," Brendan gasped. He threw his hands up before his streaming eyes. "I'm blind!"

"You're snowblind," said the Old One curtly. "It needn't be so bad. But you can't stand more light. Sit on the sled. Navarana, put a bandage over his eyes."

Brendan tried to protest, but the Old One brusquely shoved him down on the sled. "You can't stand light; I can't stand stupidity. That's how it is."

Navarana fastened a hare skin over his eyes. She whispered in his ear: "You really saw three black dots in the sky. You saw three ravens. In a moment you'll be able to hear them yourself. It means that we'll find hope when we arrive."

When the sled jerked into motion again, he was momentarily afraid of falling. But his hands were held tightly by small girls' hands.

He smiled in satisfaction and listened.

The sharp screeches came closer. He heard that the

ravens were circling above them. The screeches sounded like teasing, and the dogs howled angrily in answer.

A warm breath and a sound tickled his ear.

"Forgive me."

He was not certain whether it was her breath he heard or her words. But he grew warm with joy anyway.

ELEVEN

The ravens flew above them in the twilight.

"Fly away and show us the way to hope."

Navarana was suddenly not too tired to continue at the same quick pace.

Neither were the dogs. The ravens had given them renewed strength as well. The dogs trotted off with their curly tails erect, right behind the lead dog, which carefully sought the safest way for the sled. It was as if the dog knew that the sled was carrying a helpless burden.

The lead dog was a long-legged, muscular bitch, with a coat of blue-black and two silver-gray rings around her slanted wolflike eyes. Navarana had never had a dog like her. Toward her pups she was endlessly patient and good-natured, but the sled's team, with its seven grown males, she ruled with strict discipline. More than one stubborn young male had limped away with his tail between his legs after a bout with her powerful jaws. Her love of Navarana knew no bounds, either. She followed her everywhere, and when Navarana needed to think, the bitch could sit quietly leaning against her for hours. If Navarana was unhappy, the dog sat right in front of her and wanted to look into her eyes. The dog could stare steadily without blinking. Its black eyes were unfathomable, but Navarana felt that it knew her thoughts.

"She's the only dog I know of that will look people in the eyes," Navarana had said wonderingly to the Old One.

"That dog probably has stronger powers within it than you imagine," the Old One had answered. "The dog and the wolf are like brother and sister, and from the Ancestors' accounts, as you well know, the wolf and Human Being are related."

Her thoughts were interrupted by the lead dog's warning whine. The other dogs at once stopped behind their leader.

"She has sensed danger."

Navarana had fallen back behind the dog team. The edge of the shoreline that they followed was as even as a prairie, and she had let the dogs run without much steering. Now she saw that the sled had plunged down a slope, and she climbed in fear down to the lead dog. It was nearly dark and difficult to see.

The lead dog stood at the edge of a black chasm in the ice. It was narrow enough for the dogs to leap across but too broad for the sled to be able to cross. It would probably hurtle down into the chasm. It was deep—many, many arm-lengths deep.

They had to go around, Navarana knew that. Had to find a way farther inland. She signaled the lead dog to turn the team, but the dog did not move, just stared down into the shaft of ice with her head cocked, listening. Then she looked expectantly at Navarana.

Now Navarana heard it, too. A faint, faint gurgling sound.

"Water!" she shouted. "There's water running beneath the ice. For the first time since . . . I don't know how long!"

"We've received the second sign," said the Old One quietly. "Do you also see the third, Navarana? Out there on the horizon?"

Down at the rim of the slate-black sky, where the headland was shaped like the point of a harpoon, Navarana saw a reddish tinge. As from a campfire that someone had recently lit.

"*Aia!* Finally, I can see that the world will turn!" She

sang. "The sun will come back, and it will call the whales from the Sea's Mother. *Aiiiaaa!*" Her voice rose to a jubilant shout: "The Sea's Mother is letting the world turn!" And her tears fell freely without her caring.

Brendan suffered. Not just because his eyes were smarting as if the sockets were filled with burning coals. The worst was that he could not see all that was making Navarana so exuberantly happy. Once again he was completely helpless. Now perhaps forever blind as well.

Navarana felt his pain as keenly as if it were her own.

"I'll tell you about everything I see," she promised. "If only you'll stop feeling sorry for yourself."

She was running beside him.

"You don't need to. You've enough to do steering the sled," he answered. "And I'm not feeling sorry for myself." He tried not to be insulted by her teasing.

"But I want to tell you! I've seen the red flames of the sun! The sun always bleeds at night, and maybe it's really a springtime winter and the world will be as it was before the Hard Frost covered the sky with its black storm blanket and hid the sun."

She was out of breath and had to run for a while without talking.

Brendan could feel that the sled was moving across a

nearly flat field. There was a sharp whining beneath the whalebone runners.

"What more do you see?" he asked gently. "I can hear that we're driving across ice."

"It's fjord ice," she panted. "It's lying as thick and solid as a chain along the shore, just as it should. And it's nearly free of snow, luckily! No heavy, loose drifts of snow."

She shouted with joy, and Brendan suddenly wished that he could see her face with its high cheekbones and almond-shaped eyes. And her mouth, that soft mouth which was always so determined and stern but that he knew was beautiful when she laughed as she did now.

"There is a light farther out on the headland!" she shouted. "I see a large, round dwelling with thick smoke rising straight up and brilliant light filling the window. How beautifully it's shining through the gut skin! Someone is waiting for us, Brendan! *Aia*, what fortune! There's a large walrus skin hanging on the rack outside. It's heavy and wet and still dripping with blood."

The dogs must have caught the scent of the fresh blood, for they sped up at once, and not even the big bitch could stop the howling pack's race up the hills toward the dwelling.

Brendan felt the sled stop with a jerk, and he heard a sudden chaos of happy voices and howling dogs. It took some time before he could distinguish three unfamiliar voices, one deep and slightly grating, one soft and a little slow, and one that was as bright and light as though its owner were laughing the whole time.

The sled dogs, which were exhausted by their race and frenzied with hunger, barked madly at the strange pack of dogs undoubtedly guarding the walrus hide with their lives. He heard the hissing cracks of a whip and wild howls of pain, and the Old One shouted: "If you've enough food for our dogs, please let them have some, so we can hear ourselves think!"

"Yes, we have fresh food, for you and the dogs," laughed the three voices. "We have been waiting for you, Eldest Brother. How we've waited!"

"It wasn't possible to come before," answered the Old One apologetically. "It was necessary to wait until the time was ripe."

"You have our Little Sister along? That's good, now her final training can begin. And we'll certainly take good care of the little girls."

Brendan heard them laugh and chat as they fed the dogs. Then they fell silent while the dogs snapped up the food.

"And who is this that you've brought along, Eldest Brother?" The deep voice was serious. "I see that he is not of the family of Human Beings."

Brendan sat quietly on the sled as Navarana told how she

had found him near death in the peculiar dwelling at the strangers' ice-covered settlement. When she told about the inland ice suddenly moving, filling the cleft between the mountains and then crushing the whole settlement, he heard the three voices mumble: The ice takes everything back. That is the truth. We knew it would happen.

The Old One hurriedly said that the young man was different from other strangers, for he had a great longing to travel in the World of the Spirits. He had charms that he was guarding with his life, but only he knew their power. "He's confused," the Old One concluded, "but he's brave and willing to learn."

Brendan liked neither the Old One's paternal tone nor the sighs of the other three. He felt like the humblest of novices confronted with four strict schoolmasters.

The Old One continued by proudly telling about Navarana's polar-bear hunt, and the slow voice said, "So, Little Sister, you already know who'll be your strongest spirit guide. That makes it much easier for us to help you along the right path."

"It's bad enough that we are talking about the stranger as if he weren't here. Shall we also leave him alone to starve and freeze to death?" The bright voice was serious. "Have we forgotten our hospitality?"

Brendan felt sudden relief. He was not an outcast after all.

A warm hand touched his chin, and the bright voice continued: "Stranger, what shall we call you?"

"Brendan," he whispered.

"Brendan."

They sampled the word.

"You shall be named Akkaluq, Little Brother," said the deep voice decisively. "We'll have to see whether you merit your new name."

Brendan lay on a musk-ox hide. The long-haired fur smelled wild and sweet, and he suddenly remembered the moors at home and himself lying on his back in the sun-warmed heather, listening to the bees hum.

Heather honey is the best honey of all, his mother used to say when time hung heavy on his hands as she gathered great bunches of heather to scent and brighten everything in their little house.

"Heather is a help for everything, even bad humor," she said with a laugh.

He had loved to hear her talk like that. She had stories about everything: the open country, sea, cliffs, animals. Everything had life and magical powers, she said. Some evil and some good. But such is life. She kissed him comfortingly. "Life's not a quiet river flowing smoothly by; it's filled with rapids and quiet pools, sudden sorrows and equally sudden joys."

"Tell about the clouds," he had said. He cuddled against her warm body as she spoke.

"I see a dragon. Do you see it?" She pointed at the blue late-summer sky, where the clouds sailed like great, light feathers. "It's full and happy because it has just eaten a knight along with his armor and everything else." She suddenly laughed. "No, I shouldn't say such things, but you know I dislike those English lords. But look there, Brendan, my sweet. There you can see a boat under full sail. Do you see the whale spouting water just beneath it? That must be the whale that our pious Brendan saw. That's probably his leather boat, the one he sailed across the wild seas in on his great journey."

He nodded. He saw Brendan's boat quite clearly.

"Maybe one day you'll sail as he did. Maybe you'll be just as good as the great man whose namesake you are."

She had perhaps sensed that they would come, the lord of the manor's ironclad soldiers. He was six years old when he was thrown, kicking, across the saddle horn on that great horse and heard the captain growl: "You're in debt to your lord, slave woman. The debt must be paid. Don't whimper. You'll undoubtedly breed more."

In the fourteen years that had passed since he was abducted he had done everything to forget, everything to make the wounds heal. And he had been successful in keeping the memories at a safe distance. He had forced himself not to remember the odors, the sounds, her boundless love, and that melancholy song.

Now all the scabs were torn off, and the wounds were bleeding as if it were yesterday. He could not forgive, and he would never forget.

Navarana felt that he was crying, even if she could not hear it. Quietly, she lifted off the girls who were sleeping on her lap. She rose from her place between the three old women and the Old One and left the warm circle around the well-filled whale-oil lamp.

The youngest of the three Grandmothers, Aanaa the Youngest, looked at her and said sympathetically, "Give him a little of the puffin to eat. It's well cured and will be calming. Maybe he'll have good dreams."

Navarana nodded and went out.

The air was strangely quiet, and the dogs were resting, full and content. The sealskin, stuffed with puffin, lay up on the drying rack for fish, high above the heads of the constantly greedy dogs, now following her with their alert eyes. She climbed up, opened the skin, and carefully lifted out two fragrant bird carcasses. They were soft, nearly dissolved beneath their plumage. Her mouth was watering as she climbed down. But he was to have it all. It was exactly what he needed now, food that would fill him with warmth and an intoxicating sense of buoyancy.

He received it gratefully and ate hungrily.

She wanted to lift up the bandage over his eyes to check how everything was going, but she knew that he would not want her to see his eyes right now.

She licked her fingers and waited for him to grow sleepy.

It did not take long.

"You're my best friend," he mumbled.

He grasped her hand and squeezed. It was his first voluntary touch.

She felt it flashing through her whole body.

TWELVE

He knew that he was not sleeping, but he was not awake either. He felt no pain, and his body did not obey him when he commanded it to rise. It was dark and warm around him. A damp darkness vibrating with regular sounds, as from a giant's thudding heartbeats. He stopped struggling and allowed himself to float along with the pulsating rhythm in that enormous space which had neither up nor down. All at once he was aware of his body. It was as coolly smooth as silk and floated easily and lithely through the darkness, which was slowly growing lighter, into an intense blue color. He wanted to sing, so beautiful was the color, as no color in heaven or on earth. But he saw the shadows and knew that he had to follow soundlessly along. They glided over him, past him, and through him in an endless circular dance. Great, pliant shadows that were neither people nor animals but they did not frighten him. He wanted to be near them, in them. He had to hear their song. A song that began softly humming, that rose and rose into a mighty swell that washed through him and filled the space with light and then sank to a vibrating tone. "No!" he heard himself cry when the light waned with the song. The shadows turned slowly toward him, and he saw the Holy Mother's gentle smile, before her face vanished behind a fan of dark, gleaming hair and she disappeared with the others into the deep blue. Only their song remained, a slow dirge like the one his mother had sung when his father had been killed. And he knew that he could not follow them. In the darkness he heard a voice fill the void left behind them:

"I shall never forsake you, my son. I will always be near."

He was awakened by soft hands stroking his eyes, and he was aware of light pricking through his eyelashes.

"Sit up carefully, Akkaluq. You've slept a long time, and perhaps you can see again."

It was a voice given to laughter, and when he sat up and opened his eyes wide, he saw that she was little, round, and old, but with a glance as roguish as a young girl's.

He could see! He still saw a ring of red dots at the edge

of his vision, and his eye sockets still stung. But he could see everything around him. It was a divine miracle, and he understood what the voice had meant. He knelt down and thanked God, again and again.

They were sitting motionless when he turned, as still as four old statues, with legs crossed and eyes averted.

Brendan knelt before them. "Thank you for all you have done for me. I have no other way of showing my gratitude than this."

He took each of them by the hand and made the sign of the cross.

The silence continued. Finally, the eldest of the three women cleared her throat. Her voice was low and gravelly.

"It's our duty to save lives, Akkaluq. Life is precious in the Land of the Human Beings, for we're few in our clan and the road is short to a sudden and cruel death. Life is just a thin membrane dividing the living from the World of the Dead. But the World of the Living is indispensable, for it's through it that we're all reborn and can rectify our sins against the Mother of all life."

"The *Father* of all life," said Brendan at last.

This was a moment he had known would have to arrive. Once he had looked forward to making all heathens into God's Christian children. But that was earlier, an eternity ago, when he had sat in the monastery in England listening to the priests versed in the Scriptures discussing the Church's mission in the uncivilized parts of the world. Back then he had not doubted that they were right, they who maintained that wild heathens did not have souls. They did not even resemble civilized people, for their skin was burned and their bodies headless, and no one knew whether they could speak through the mouths in their chests and, if so, whether it was Satan's voices one would hear.

The discussions between the priests had often been heated, for there were those who deeply disagreed. One of them was Brother Gareth, the monastery's librarian. He was the brother who had studied the most writings of every kind, including those in languages other than Latin.

"What proof do you have that this is true?" Brother Gareth had said angrily. "I've read Roman, Greek, and Arabic accounts from journeys to the most distant lands of the known world. Those travelers have met peculiar beings and animals, and they've seen astonishing countries and cities. But none of them say that their people have met headless heathens. Neither do the Icelandic skalds recount that. They tell peculiar things about the wild heathens on Greenland, but they've never mentioned that they are headless. Brothers, isn't it dangerous to fill the minds of young monks with such frightening accounts? Should not our inexperienced Brother Brendan, whom Our Holy Father in Rome has selected, receive something more edifying on his journey to that horribly cold land?"

"What proofs are stronger than the testimony to be found here in Hereford, noted by one of our dear departed brothers?" The abbot's voice cut through the room like a knife.

All eyes had immediately turned back to the old map, where headless heathens and even more peculiar animals were clearly drawn on the unknown parts of the world.

"Our long-deceased brother never traveled there himself. We know that. The map was drawn by him here in Hereford according to the accounts of seafarers!" Brother Gareth answered. "And we all know that seafarers are known for their exaggerations."

But Brendan had seen that he was perspiring. For Brother Gareth knew, as did all the others, that the most sacred duty for the old abbot was to do battle against heretics, skeptics, and heathens.

"Do you trust more in the accounts of disbelievers than in those of our Holy Church's faithful servants?" The abbot's voice was extremely low, and everyone in the room had the same thought: Watch your tongue, Brother Gareth, or you may lose it.

Brendan had left for Greenland without thinking more about the conflict between those learned men. He had not seen any heathens, and no one he met talked about them. The few Northmen that were still alive had enough to worry about with their own misfortunes. They would rather talk about why the ships had stopped coming from Iceland, Norway, and Europe than about headless heathens. Brendan had enough work to do and much to think about. He had no reasonable explanation as to why the Holy Father in Rome had closed down the bishopric at Gardar. That had happened nearly a hundred years earlier, but it was still looked upon as a betrayal that had accelerated the misfortune that had stricken the populace of Northmen in the country. Neither could Brendan explain why Pope Nicholas had waited so long to send priests and monks to save Christianity's farthest outpost.

But Brendan remembered well his fear when he awoke from his deathlike torpor in the church and saw Navarana for the first time. And he remembered the shame he had felt as she helped him back to life. Then he began to doubt what the men of the Church had impressed upon him. His doubt had grown even stronger after his apprenticeship with the Old One. Now he was uncertain whether his preaching would be powerful and convincing enough.

But he said aloud, "My God is the only true and almighty God. God is the creator of the world and rules over heaven and earth. Everything is God's work: the light, the sea, the land, the animals, and the plants. God gave humans souls and made them masters over the animals. And He bade humans to live according to His commandments and to renounce the Devil and all his works. On the Day of Judgment God shall judge the living and the dead and determine who shall have eternal life."

They stared at him. Long and questioningly. Then they looked at one another, and he knew that they had discussed all this while he was sleeping.

Aanaa the Youngest spoke first.

"Your faith is different from ours."

"My faith is the only true one. God is the only true God," he repeated.

The Old One moved uneasily and cleared his throat.

"Brendan, I got to know you when you were helpless and alone. You've shared my dwelling, and I've given you knowledge just as if you belonged to the family of Human Beings."

"You've treated me as if I were your grandson," said Brendan meekly. "You know that I'm grateful! But . . ."

"But? Still you say that my faith is worth less than yours? That you, who've lived for only a short time and who didn't have the sense to live as a Human Being, have the only true faith? How can you who don't even know our faith reject it so easily?"

He was breathing deeply.

Brendan could hear that he was agitated, but his face was expressionless when he continued: "Where was your God when you were suffering the worst, Stranger? And where was he when Navarana forced you to leave behind your precious, heavy idol?"

His words felt like lashes from a whip.

Brendan grew mute with despair.

It was not supposed to be like this! Nothing was as simple as the abbot had said it would be. God's words were to open heathen hearts, the abbot had assured everyone. The heathens would fall to their knees and meekly give thanks for their salvation; thereafter, they would happily allow themselves to be baptized. How was he supposed to baptize these old people who had such an unshakable faith themselves and who felt his preaching was an insult?

"Your preaching must be like a flaming sword, for conversion is a holy war against Satan and all his works," the abbot would have said. "Your faith must be as firm as a rock and your will like the sharply honed blade of a sword. Never believe that heathens and the wayward know what is best for them."

But the abbot had never left the monastery. He was much too concerned with the holy crusades and brooding over the steady spread of sin in spite of the Church's great efforts to punish sinners and heretics. The abbot had never tried to convert heathens. But if he had been in Brendan's place, he would surely have said that the heathens' faith was Satan's work.

Brendan felt a light hand on his shoulder. He looked up. Aanaa the Eldest looked deep into his eyes. Her eyes sparkled with laughter.

"Don't lose heart, Akkaluq. Fight for your faith, and be assured that we would like to learn everything about you and your world. We've long known that Human Beings are not alone in the world. Neither are we alone in having a faith. You're the first person we've met with a faith that's completely different from our own. We would like to hear about your god, understand how your amulets work, and know what the tasks of your shamans are. But we must listen to each other's faiths and treat their differences with respect."

Never had he been forgiven like this, not even among the mildest of the brothers in the monastery. He thought ashamedly: I learned to love my own faith but not to respect others'. First I must learn about their faith before I convert them to my own.

They said no more, and he was relieved. He had been wrong, and he needed time to think. He would have to preach God's message in some other way. Without wounding their pride, without losing their trust. For he could no longer be without them, without her.

Navarana was standing out on the harpoonlike tip of the headland. She was humming contentedly as she worked. She had been idle for such a long time. So, too, had the women's big boat, the *umiak*, which she was busy repairing. There was nothing the matter with the skeleton of the boat. It was made of well-saturated driftwood and securely bound and fastened with pegs of narwhal tooth. But the heavy walrus hide that was pulled tightly around the boat's frame had cracked in many places. She wanted to repair the boat, for she was now certain that it would soon be in use again.

The world would finally turn. The sky was still as gray as the inside of a whale-oil lamp, but she saw that its color was paler and speckled in some places with blue, and the sun was a pale yellow disk that did not quite disappear. It was almost impossible to believe. After innumerable days and nights of darkness and biting cold she saw the light rising carefully, tentatively, as if it did not yet dare to trust itself.

"Just come," she hummed. "Just come forth, and I will sing in Your honor, for You are the Mother of all life."

She turned her glance toward the sea. The ice was still like a hard shell, but she could hear that the icebergs had begun to rock uneasily. With sharp, dry, wonderful cracking sounds that could only mean they would soon be able to sail again. The wind from the south, which was chasing the sea mist like great, silent birds, was mild. It carried the promising scent of the changes that were coming. The world was again beautiful and wondrous, and she felt how deeply she had missed it.

The three ravens sat a little to one side, following her work with shining eyes. Navarana smiled. They reminded her of three wise women who wanted to make certain that she was doing everything right but who did not want to show that they were meddling. Three grandmothers, each with twin souls, she thought. Three great shamans who had strengthened her belief that the world could be turned and who were her generous teachers.

The snow crunched behind her. She turned and saw Brendan coming. Carefully, clumsily, as if each step were perilous, but he walked without help and had borrowed the Old One's sun protector. It was beautifully carved from whale bone and fit his eyes like a little mask.

"Don't look toward the light," she called. "Look at something dark. Look at me and the boat."

He sat down heavily beside her.

"What's the matter?" She knew that something was bothering him.

"I have erred," he said at last.

She looked questioningly at him, but he did not continue.

Perhaps he could not yet find words for all that was new, she thought, and turned back to her work. "You can help me. Then you'll be doing something useful."

"Gladly." He got up immediately.

She showed him how to hold the pieces of leather so they were stretched tight while she sewed. She also let him soften the sinew thread with his teeth.

"It's women's work," she said apologetically. "But we're too few to bother about that now. Besides, you'll learn how to save your life in a kayak that's been torn by the ice, and that's very useful."

She explained eagerly, and he listened. But she knew that his attention was somewhere else.

"What's the matter?"

It was a difficult question to ask, for when people are terribly burdened by something, one should wait a long time before intruding. The best thing was to play or dance with someone who was burdened by heavy thoughts. But he was not a Human Being; therefore, he would perhaps think her impolite. She waited.

"It's . . . ," he began. Then it became impossible to continue.

Navarana looked at him uneasily. For some reason she

suddenly thought of the mountain she had once seen in the south of the Land of the Human Beings. A mountain that had been as black and still as all other mountains but that had suddenly opened up with a thundering crack. Tremendous flames poured out from the mountaintop, and the sky was covered with black clouds of smoke. The flames had become rivers of glowing fire, and the ice had steamed for many days afterward. She still remembered her terror and surprise that what had looked like a completely ordinary mountain was hiding such staggering power.

"Don't leave me," he said, suddenly pleading. "I've no one else but you. But I'm unable to explain, for not even you can comprehend."

He could not bear to tell her about his shame and betrayal. About the awful feeling of having humiliated the Old One and the three women and simultaneously of having failed his loving God.

"I no longer know myself." The words came from afar, as from someone outside himself. "I know only chaos. Everything that was safe and solid before is like a thin crust above a deep chasm. It's abominable. I'm abominable."

She took off her mitten and let her fingers slowly brush across his cheek. Her fingers became damp and warm.

They sat silently for a long time. Beside them the ravens

kept guard. Behind them the dogs were dozing. From the snow-clad dwelling they heard the drums singing.

"You need to meet your spirits and get help," she said quietly. "Do you hear the drums? They're traveling now, my grandmothers and the Old One. They'll explore the world and decide what my task will be. While you slept, they drummed, and I met the sow for the third time. Now she's my strongest spirit guide."

Navarana took a deep breath and continued: "She did not mind your wearing her pelt."

Now it was said.

He smiled gratefully. Then he grew sad again.

"You must go out alone and wait for your spirits," she said urgently. "You must struggle. You must expose yourself to great hardships. You must renounce and endure; you must believe and withstand. Through the drum, song, and dance, the trance came to me, and I flew like a bird without wings."

"In a darkness that has no up or down and no end," he continued. He trembled. "I've seen it."

"My friend," she whispered. "Go out and find your spirit guide and yourself."

THIRTEEN

It was a long time since anyone had said anything, but the silence was not painful. They were just engrossed in their thoughts. They had eaten well of the seal that the youngest grandmother had caught. It had been large and fat, and all the reddish yellow blubber, the meat, and the broth tasted delicious.

Navarana could not remember ever before having been full all the time. It was a new experience not to feel hunger but to have a strange sense of peace.

"You know that many in our family believe that hunger makes the best hunter," the Old One began, as if he had heard her thoughts.

She listened.

"But that's a dangerous belief, for many reasons. Hunger does terrible things to people. It kills with cruel pains, not like the frost, which entices one into a numbing sleep. Hunger is particularly hard on children. Those of our children who survive hunger are never quite the same again."

They heard the girls outside laughing and playing with the pups of Navarana's lead dog.

Navarana knew that he wanted to tell her something important, but she was not certain what it was. She listened more attentively.

"Hungry people are capable of doing anything in order to appease their hunger," he continued. "When hunger torments a settlement, everyone becomes everyone else's enemy. Friends steal from friends, children rob their parents, and the weakest are killed without mercy."

Navarana gasped. At once she knew where he was heading, and she remembered everything clearly, the dreadfulness that she had so long suppressed.

That long winter, the storms that would never die down, the hunters who came home empty-handed or who did not come home at all. Her father had kept his hunting luck longer than anyone else, while enmity grew between him and his elder brother. They had danced the drum dances and sung insulting ditties about each other to try to settle their struggle in a peaceful way, but nothing was made better by her father's always winning the song contests.

Then her father also lost his hunting luck, and hunger began to gnaw at everyone in earnest.

Navarana could still remember the dread she had felt of her father's being killed or of losing her own life. Hunger had forced them to eat all the dogs and, after that, to fight over old sealskin buckets, which could be boiled and chewed, and whale-oil lamps, which could be licked clean of old grease.

Anything, anything was possible, she knew. And the very worst happened.

Her uncle, who grew steadily more angry and evil, started the rumor that her gentle mother was the cause of all their misfortune. She had refused to observe the taboos, the uncle maintained. And he received support from the power-hungry shaman, who had long lusted for Navarana but who had been rejected by both her mother and father. When he started claiming that he had evidence that her mother was an evil sorceress planning to send murderous *tupilaqs* against the seal hunters, Navarana and her father knew that anything might happen. Her father and mother tried everything to regain trust at the settlement, but they were all bewitched by dread. Her father began to spend more and more time out on the ice, but his hunting luck did not return.

One day, soon after he had set out on yet another lengthy search for game, her uncle and two hunters arrived, led by the shaman. Without saying a word, they grabbed her mother and dragged her out. Navarana and her two little sisters ran after them, begging them to leave their mother alone. But the shaman just growled that it was the punishment she deserved. Then her mother shook herself free and said proudly, "I will go on my own. If only my child will follow me to the edge."

Still Navarana could not bring herself to think of the moment when her mother stood on the edge of that precipitous gorge where ice floes in the fjord far below were butting heavily together. "I am innocent," she had said. "But if this must happen for you to live in peace, I will do it." The echo of Navarana's own screams and those of her sisters resounded again and again in the cold gorge and in her dreams.

"Of course it hurts, Little Sister." Aanaa the Eldest hugged her. "But hidden memories must be brought out into the light, otherwise your life can be poisoned by vengeance. Is that the reason you began seeking the force outside yourself?"

She nodded.

"It was good that you let us see why. You cannot go forward with poisoned feelings. We'll help you attain great power, but we can't risk your using the power for harm and not for good. You must forget vengeance now. Both for your own sake, since it will make you vulnerable in a meeting with evil spirits, and for your mother's sake. Do you think that she would want her sacrifice to ruin your life?"

Navarana had never thought about it like that. She had always thought of revenge as a necessity. But she knew that Aanaa was right. It was a relief to be able to forget revenge, but it was a feeling as unfamiliar to her as having a full stomach.

"Thank you," she said.

"You've all but finished your training," said Aanaa the Next Oldest, satisfied.

She poured more broth into the cups.

Navarana drank, enjoying the taste of the glowing stone that had warmed the soup.

"He's doing as well as he can with himself and his spirits."

The Old One gave her a sidelong glance.

"I wasn't thinking about him at all." Navarana could feel that she was blushing. "He has only been away for two days and two nights."

"Maybe we'll play the put-out-the-light game when he returns." Aanaa the Youngest chuckled teasingly. "We're certainly not too old to play with a young man!"

"No! He wants no one to touch him!"

Navarana could have bitten her tongue. This was something she had not even allowed herself to think.

"I see," smiled the Old One. "Then we'll talk no more about it."

He was suddenly serious. "You should know that we're pleased by all he has told us about his spirits. His accounts are new and strange, and much is difficult to comprehend. But his conviction about their heaven and hell is strong, as is his love for his Father God and his son who gave his life to save their world. His explanation of the world's order is certainly different from ours. We can still learn a lot, and maybe we'll all be changed by it."

"I'm just worried that he still doesn't know the demons he will have to conquer. Least of all those hiding within himself."

Brendan's demons? Navarana waited tensely for Aanaa the Youngest to continue. What did she know that Navarana had not discovered? Brendan was insecure, and he disliked himself. Navarana had certainly felt it. But she could not grasp that he was hiding demons.

Aanaa the Youngest explained no more. But the mystery remained hanging unclarified between her and Navarana, and suddenly Navarana remembered the Old One's words: Think for yourself. Don't blindly obey. Don't trust everything you are told.

The three Grandmothers were like great spirits to her. Maybe she needed to be reminded that even shamans were ordinary people.

Aanaa the Youngest seized the drum and closed her eyes.

The drumming began quite slowly, then rose into a mighty wave that soon washed over Navarana, and she let herself drift happily along with the song.

The Grandmothers sang the winds' song. From the depths of their throats the winds sounded from North, West, South, and East. The Grandmothers were the winds and knew what the winds intended.

We will never stop blowing, for our work stretches from the dawn of time to eternity. One day the Human Beings will learn to live with us; one day they will stop dreaming themselves away from us. We will always be here keeping the world together whenever they awake.

It continued all night, and Navarana flew with them to settlements in all parts of the Land of the Human Beings, and everywhere she saw despair. Then she knew why they were giving the quest to her.

"Am I really the right one?" she asked, and they showed her that they trusted her. She rejoiced in all the spirit guides they gave her and was saddened that they would leave her.

She flew until her wings touched the sun.

It was late in the morning when she heard the stamping outside.

She arose from the sleeping bench and went out.

He smiled, and his eyes were as blue as a summer sky.

She did not need to ask.

"I found the light," he said quietly. "Finally."

They spent several days preparing. There was much that could not be said, much that they had to consider, individually and together.

Brendan asked little about where they were going, but a lot about practical things, like how to make harpoon points and tie nets. It was as if he had to convince the Old One that he was equal to the task.

"I have a gift for you," said Brendan to the Old One.

"Where?" The Old One was as curious as a small boy.

"In my head," answered Brendan secretively.

He found a piece of old gut skin that had been used for a window and brought sticks that he had gathered. The sticks he put in the lamp and burned them slowly into charcoal.

The Old One waited.

"Look." Brendan slowly started to draw lines on the skin. "Here is my name, here is yours, and here is Navarana's."

"Wonderful!" The Old One grew short of breath in his eagerness to learn.

"What do you call this gift?"

Brendan drew the whole alphabet before he answered.

"Writing," he said proudly. "It's different from the art of singing, but with these letters you can secure everything you're thinking and remembering on stone or bone or skin. And you can be far away when someone finds what you've written, and they'll read your thoughts exactly as you've thought them."

"Teach me everything about your art of writing."

There was not enough time, but Brendan told how the letters expressed many different languages and how people in distant lands and centuries had written thick books filled with thoughts, still just as vivid as when they were first conceived. He spoke at length about the Holy Scriptures, which were a revelation from God and the basis for his entire faith, and then he told about Brother Gareth, who lovingly gathered all the books in the monastery's library, even books with thoughts that were different from those that the abbot liked.

For an instant he wondered whether he ought to tell the Old One about the controversy over heathens between those versed in the Scriptures, but he let it be. He did not want to offend the Old One. He did not want to reveal the foolishness of his own world, either.

"Our arts are extremely different," said the Old One. "As you know, the wisdom and experiences of Human Beings are preserved in songs and tales. They're our most precious inheritance from the Ancestors. We know that the tales are as old as the memory of Human Beings and that we've no more important task on this earth than to keep the tales alive. If we didn't pass them on from generation to generation, Human Beings would soon disappear. I thank you for this great gift, Akkaluq. Our inheritance will be even safer through your art of writing. Tell me now more about the dwellings full of books."

And Brendan told all he knew.

The Old One thought for a long time before he spoke. "That's a beautiful account. I would like to see your books. It may be that I'll not use your art of writing in books," he said almost apologetically, "for they demand a great deal of hide and are heavy to carry on journeys. But I will always bear the art of writing in my memory and use it in such a way as is sensible for us." He smiled broadly. "I've never received a gift like this before. You've truly enriched me."

"You've made me richer than you can guess," answered Brendan sincerely. "Never have I had a teacher like you."

They looked at each other. Both felt the same sorrow and happiness.

The Old One stuck his hand inside his coat and took an amulet out of his pouch.

"This shall be yours now," he said. "It's my most powerful amulet."

It was a large, milk-white tooth, as sharp and as pointed as a knife. "The creature has a great black fin that cuts the waves like a knife. You'll recognize it when you see it, for it is the sea's fastest and most dangerous whale. Our family in the north that hunts it most calls it the wolf whale, for in the songs of their Ancestors it is said that it once hunted on land like a wolf. It hunts just as mercilessly as the wolf, but it also has the whale's gentleness, and like all animals," he smiled, "it has the soul of a Human Being. All the same, you need never fear the killer whale, for it's now also your *Tornarssuq*, your greatest and mightiest spirit guide. It'll show you the way and protect you always."

"You'll always be with us," thought Brendan.

The Old One nodded.

They both knew it was so.

FOURTEEN

The black fin had followed them for a long time.

At first it was just a tiny triangle far out in the broad channel of water that had suddenly opened up in the enormous mass of drifting ice.

When she first saw the channel of water, nearly transparent in the light from the sun attempting to break through the layer of clouds, she thought that her eyes were playing tricks on her. The three of them had traveled quite far without seeing a sign of life. It was difficult to believe that it actually was the fin of a whale out there. It could well be an illusion, for one moment the fin was there, the next it was gone. Besides, it was not moving the way whales did.

It's only ice, Navarana said decisively to herself. Just one of those clear, treacherous ice spurs that hunters don't discover until their kayaks are sliced by its sharp edges. It's a miracle that the ocean currents have finally conquered the pack ice and sprung open a channel of water. It would be expecting too much of the Sea's Mother to have also sent a whale.

So she thought. But she continued to see it, even if she refused to believe that it existed.

She noticed how tired she was of traveling. It felt as if she had done nothing but load the sled, feed the dogs, hitch them up, trot behind or beside the sled until darkness fell, and then try to find a place to rest for the night. She had lost count of how many days they had traveled, but it seemed forever. There was hardly time to eat or think and definitely no time to talk to Brendan. She was exhausted and sick of it. She knew that he must be much worse off, he who was not born to the Human Beings' harsh life, he who also had not received from the Old One and the Grandmothers a task that had to be carried out in a hurry. He said nothing, and Navarana was happy about that, even though she had a bad conscience for not explaining more about the islands, fjords, mountains, and plateaus, about the empty coastal and inland hunting grounds, where generations of Human Beings had lived from time immemorial. Brendan did not complain; he accepted his share of the work, and she noticed that he was driving the sled dogs as well and as safely as she did herself.

The sled they were using was larger than her own, for the Grandmothers thought they should bring the women's boat. The *umiak* was so large that there was plenty of room for the sled, gear, and dogs, and it was sensible to take it along. No one could know how solid the ice would be across the bay between the northwesterly point of Greenland and the Land of the Human Beings in the northwest. They could row the boat if they could not use the sled. But the boat made the sled heavier and more difficult to maneuver, and the dogs and Brendan and she herself all grew steadily more exhausted from trying to maintain the same fast pace.

Navarana well remembered that long trip by sled when her father and she and her sisters had traveled from the settlement in the northwest to southern Greenland. Now she was grateful that she remembered everything so clearly, for it was difficult to steer according to the landmarks that the Old One had told her about. It was ages since he had traveled that distance, long before the Hard Frost had changed the landscape so completely. When the Old One had traveled, he had also been able to steer by the stars in the evening sky. But no stars showed the way for Navarana. She tried to follow her father's advice: Keep close to the land. It was safe, for there long reaches of the ice were solid and almost smooth, but it meant that they often had to make strenuous detours.

"Heed the wind; it can help you keep your direction," her father had said. She had not thought she would ever need that advice, for as long as Pitoraq and his demons sent winds in all directions, it was impossible to steer according to the wind. But Pitoraq had now withdrawn to the inland ice, and it did not look as if he would bother them again. The winds were now blowing as usual, and she knew how long she could rely on them. It was a good change. The other important change was the cold. It continued to be cold. Vastly colder than it ought to be. But the cold was at least constant, without extreme fluctuations that made tears spurt and the body shake as if with fever. They could now clothe themselves for the cold, for she knew how long it would remain constant during the day.

On the whole there was enough to rejoice about, Navarana thought, suddenly realizing how pessimistic she had become. It was because she was too exhausted to really notice the changes, probably also because she hoped for too much.

Each time they crossed a fjord or traveled past a high cliff, she hoped. Seals used to frolic in the fjords, and auks and puffins used to teem on the cliffs. But the fjords were deserted and the cliffs glazed with ice, and the sun had not changed. It smoldered each morning like a little campfire on the horizon but still was quickly extinguished behind heavy layers of cloud.

The Grandmothers had given them enough food to manage with for some time. They did not yet need to worry about the hunting grounds' being desolate. Still, they were extremely careful. Only the dogs got what they needed, for without the dogs her journey and quest were impossible. But their food could not last forever, and Navarana thought constantly about what they would do when it was gone.

"I would so have liked to give you my hunting song," Aanaa the Youngest had said when Navarana was ready to leave. She herself needed only to sit on the ice and sing for a seal to come and gladly give up its life to her, for she and the two other Grandmothers knew the World of the Spirits and the World of the Dead extremely well. Better almost than they knew the World of the Living.

"You probably need to find your own song, Navarana. It takes time, but you have the power. Just trust that you have it."

But the Grandmothers possessed great magic. Navarana had not yet dared to see if she could charm, for she was afraid of failing. And as of yet it was not necessary to test whether her power was strong enough, she thought. But she knew that it was dangerous to postpone the attempt. No one could tell what might occur. The sled could suddenly fall into a hidden fissure or they could lose the dogs. Anything was possible in this severe landscape. It was foolish to be unprepared for survival. She knew that her common sense was right, but it only made her sadder.

Meanwhile she continued to see the fin of the whale emerge at the far side of the channel of water, and she continued to tell herself that it was merely an ice spur. But one day it came much closer. Against her will, her heart began to hammer with excitement. It was unmistakable, that fine, sharply curved triangle. It *was* a fin that was slicing out of the water and disappearing, first for long periods before the whale appeared, inhaling in long drags, then in short, snorting turns. Only the killer whale swam in this way to breathe.

"Of course I see it," said Brendan. "It's been following us."

He said it as if it were the most natural thing in the world that the sea's proudest hunter should follow them.

She wanted to say, Why haven't you said anything before! But she checked herself. She had not cared about anything but her exhausted body and her disappointment over the changes being less than she had hoped.

Instead, she said, almost annoyed, "The killer whale is the only sea animal that eats meat. It's a true predator that can also be dangerous to Human Beings, did you know that?" The last part she was not at all sure of.

"I know." Brendan suddenly smiled broadly. "I also know that the killer whale is just as much wolf as whale and that its soul is much like a person's."

She just stared, unsure whether he was joking with her.

"I've learned that you shouldn't just listen to a tale but also digest it." He was serious now. "When you digest a tale, it becomes a part of you and you become a part of the tale. Isn't that true?"

"It's quite true."

She was speechless. Something had changed him. It was beyond anything she had believed possible. An adult stranger had been transformed into a Human Being, and the transformation had occurred through his own will and not through magic.

"I told you that I've seen my light."

He said nothing more.

Days passed before anything happened.

Then one morning, soon after they had loaded the tent on the sled and were ready to start, the beautiful fin came much closer and they saw the supple arch of the whale's back. Immediately the lead dog began to howl longingly and without cease, as if she were wailing at the moon. She turned and looked at Navarana, and Navarana knew that the dog could not be budged.

"We must go on, Wolf Sister," she shouted. But for all her coaxing and commanding, the bitch sat just as immovably as before, staring toward the fin, large and shiny, cutting through the quiet water, coming steadily closer to them.

"She's waiting," said Brendan quietly. "We ought to do the same."

Then it happened. The great, glistening body of the whale shot out of the water like an arrow and turned in the air. They saw its black head with a mouth that looked as if it were smiling, the oval white spot above the little eye, and the soft belly, white as snow. In a sparkling rain of droplets the whale dove again and everything became completely silent.

"Sing the song," said Brendan quickly. "You know it. Sing it now! Ask it to come back and give us something to eat from its catch."

And she sang, first hesitantly, then more fervently. Immediately the calm surface of the water opened again, and they saw the whale's great tail rise up, high and ever higher in the air. Then with enormous power its tail hit the water, and the spray rose up to the sky. When the waves finally settled, they saw the seal down below them on the edge of the ice. It was bloody and torn, as if the whale had been devouring its prey when her song called it.

Navarana and Brendan stood still without daring to move. It was almost unbelievable.

"Thank you, Great God," mumbled Brendan.

"Thank you, Great Mother," mumbled Navarana.

Both of them knew that they owed the Old Ones their thanks.

After that, Navarana no longer worried about food. She did not wonder why the whale now swam ahead of them, either. But each morning they both greeted the whale, and the whole day they followed the whale's movements just as closely as it followed them.

One day it was no longer alone. They saw two fins, the second a little smaller but just as beautifully arched as the first. The whales were swimming in precisely the same rhythm, diving and cutting their way up from the water as if they were of one breath.

They stopped the sled and sat breathlessly following what was happening. The whales rushed through the water at enormous speed; then they turned sharply and came straight at them in ever-narrowing circles. All at once, in a cloud of rainbow-colored water, they shot up into the air, their great tails quivering above the surface of the water. Their mighty bodies met, and for a moment black and white melted together before they dove in a great arc down into the depths. The whales were gone for a long time, but the waves clearly showed that they were still there, playing together just beneath the water's surface. Just as suddenly as they had disappeared, they ripped through the water again, and the couple saw the male's arrow-shaped black marking pointing straight at his red sex organ, and they saw the female's sexual opening swollen and red in the white marking of her belly. For a dizzying moment the whales were united, and their beautiful song reverberated over the water long after they had disappeared again.

Brendan and Navarana sat transfixed.

Both had felt the whales' intoxication. Both sensed the excitement vibrating between them. Neither of them was able to look into the other's eyes.

Brendan remembered again the Old One's last admonition. He had spoken for some time about the taboos that had to be observed and the respect that had to be shown for the Sea's Mother and her creatures. "Remember that you shall not desire Navarana."

Alarmed, Brendan had assured him that desire had never been in his thoughts, for he had taken a vow of eternal celibacy to the Lord, and he had not thought of breaking it.

"Good," the Old One had said with his inscrutable smile.

Since then Brendan had done all he could not to see her supple neck; her eyes, which smiled even when she was furious; and the arc of her stomach, which was always visible when she stretched.

When they were about to lie down for the night in the little tent, on opposite sides of the whale-oil lamp, he had turned away, to escape seeing all that caused his stomach muscles to contract in uncontrollable joy. And every evening he carved *Mea Culpa* in capital letters on the inside of his eyelids to protect himself against his dreams.

"We have to get on," she said abruptly. Her voice was stern.

He nodded gratefully.

They drove the dogs and themselves harder than usual that day. The whole time the whales were there showing the way, but now neither of them dared to look toward the sea.

It was late in the evening when they finally stopped. They had come around a headland and suddenly saw a winter dwelling on a small rocky ledge above the edge of the shore. It was the first dwelling they had seen that was not completely buried in ice and snow, and they decided to spend the night in it. Inside, the walls were covered in glistening frost. Clearly no people had been there for some time. It was not large enough for a family, but Navarana guessed that it had been built by coastal hunters who could return often to a very good hunting area.

"This has probably been a good hunting ground with lots of animals, both walrus and seal." She was glad that she had found something ordinary to say, for she had immediately seen that there was only one sleeping bench in the dwelling. It was too late to turn back.

"And there's a fine, large hearth," said Brendan. "I'll gather fuel." He stood outside swallowing for a time without finding a reasonable excuse for setting up the tent.

"Lord, give me strength," he prayed.

But he knew that this was a trial that God expected him to manage alone.

He spent a terribly long time finding the hard-packed dry sod and walrus bones that would burn the whole night.

For the first time in ages, the sky was only partially overcast. The northern lights washed across the sky in great multicolored flames. It was so beautiful that it almost took his breath away. But for some strange reason it just made him think of her even more.

Neither of them could say afterward exactly how it happened or which of them took the first step. It was as if they acted unconsciously. But when they melted together, they were both aware that it was this they had longed for. They were awake the whole night, each discovering the pleasure and intimacy of the other. When they finally had no more strength, they lay entwined, mouth to mouth.

Navarana was half asleep when she heard Brendan laugh. She raised her head.

"You know," he said, his fingers playing with her hair, "the last admonition I received from the Old One was not to desire you. I had no idea that I've been desiring you my entire life."

"Did he really say that?"

He nodded.

"The old fox! Whenever he has wanted me to do something, he has warned me against it. 'Very few women have become shamans.' He knew that I would strive all the more to become one. 'Don't try to struggle against destiny.' He knew that I would struggle even harder."

"He knew that we are alike," said Brendan quietly.

"Alike and quite different." She smiled teasingly. "Black and white, with different parts that fit together perfectly."

"You're my life, do you know that?"

She nodded mutely.

"That was what I meant when you asked what I found. I

found that my love of God and my love of you are of the same kind. My life is His and yours."

Gently, she leaned over him.

"Our roots have grown together and can no longer be divided. We're still two, but we can bear one fruit."

FIFTEEN

As soon as they understood that they belonged together, they decided to marry. Navarana wanted them to remain for a time in the hunters' tiny dwelling, so that she could prepare them both for the marriage.

Brendan was grateful. He wanted to seal their covenant there where it had been made, and he needed peace to think. He was more exhausted than ever before in his life. Not only from the long days of travel but from the changes. Changes that also resembled a journey taking him ever farther from the person he had once been. The Brendan who had come to Greenland with his head filled with confident opinions and great dreams was distant and almost unreal. Now he was not certain who he was or where he was going.

He had a feeling of being alien to himself, with a life like a blank page. The thought of chaos was frightening, and he needed calm in which to tell God everything, for only He could understand Brendan's torment.

It was not his love of Navarana that worried Brendan. The changes he faced had not shaken his faith, either. On the contrary, he was now experiencing a greater intimacy with God than ever before, with a supremely loving Heavenly Father who was within him and with him in everything. It was the Church's teaching and the abbot's command that Brendan felt he had betrayed. He had not managed to baptize the Old One, and he could never bring himself to force Navarana to relinquish her faith. Brendan knew that they would live well together even if their faiths were different, but in all his dreams he heard the abbot's strict voice, and he knew that his disobedience would never be forgiven. *Lord, deliver me from the abbot's wrath!* he prayed, but God answered as he had expected: *You chose to go your own way. You must learn to live with your conscience. Be grateful that it is roused.*

It became impossible for him to think without anguish of life in the monastery. He felt guilty for his disobedience with regard to the task he had received and viewed with increasing aversion much of what he had learned and blindly believed. When he began to doubt and to think for himself, he looked at his former life in an entirely different way. What had earlier been definite and real now seemed as unreal as a dream. At once Brendan knew that he could never return to the monastery. For the first time he felt stranded.

I am with you, he knew that God was saying.

He still had to find himself.

Navarana was worried. She had no idea what kind of struggle was taking place within him, but she understood that he had lost his footing. He wanted to be close to her, but he was not present. For hours he stared into the flames of the whale-oil lamp, but she knew that there he saw only darkness. That was how she had seen him at the Grandmothers', locked within himself. Then she had asked him to go out to meet his spirits. Now she asked him to take over her task of waiting on the shore to sing for the whales until they came with their prey.

Brendan agreed, to please her, but at first he could think of nothing but his feeling of emptiness. He had to make an effort to concentrate on that enormous body that would shoot out of the water to deliver its prey. Then, almost imperceptibly, the wait changed. Each time he managed to predict where the whale's fin would cut through the water, it felt like a victory. When he heard the whale's first snorting exhalation, he sang for it with greater sincerity. The wait became an obsession, even though he knew that the whales would always come with their prey. When he came back to Navarana with a seal or fish, he was often so exhausted that he wished only to sleep. But his sleep was uneasy, for in his dreams he relived the wait, only with a greater urgency than in real life. He heard his own chilled breathing and felt his fingers growing numb in his mittens. He felt the creaking of the ice, which meant that the temperature was changing; he felt the wind blowing and knew that if it came from the north, it would be impossible for him to wait. He always awoke dissatisfied with himself. There was something he still had not seen, still did not really understand. He spent more and more of his waiting brooding over why he felt inadequate. It took time before he understood that the reason was his nearness to nature.

Never in his adult life had Brendan imagined nature as a living being. Earlier he had never noticed that the mountains spoke to him, that the sea had a story to tell that he could hear with his senses. For years, Brendan had not used, or bothered about, his senses. Of course, he had memories of fragrances and sights and tastes and the touch of fingers. But those were memories belonging to his childhood in Ireland, a time spent in happy ignorance of adult life. In the monastery he had devoted all his time to prayer and meditation, fasting and self-denial, hard work in the fields and study of the Holy Scriptures. It was a life in which surroundings were unimportant and experiences of nature merely diverted attention from spiritual experience.

From the moment his senses awakened, he saw how uniquely beautiful this harsh land was. He longed to sit quietly among the blue-black mountains, for each day the cold carved fantastic new patterns in the furrowed mountainsides. Beyond the shore ice, the channel ran with open water. When the temperature rose slightly, great floes broke loose from the hard-packed edge of ice and floated out into the channel. The drifting ice floes resembled frozen angels with outspread wings, and he knew that God was present. When the ice drifted away, he saw that the channel was a little broader and the water more mysteriously green. He knew that he was seeing the transformations that Navarana was waiting for, and he often remained sitting until it was completely dark, so that he might have as much as possible to tell her. Each morning, as soon as the first pale red tint appeared on the horizon, he went out to experience the new transitions.

One morning there was a great iceberg mirrored in the channel. The reflection of the towering iceberg was perfect in every detail. He saw the steep side of the iceberg and knew its sharp edges meant that the iceberg had recently torn itself loose from the inland ice. He knew that its shiny mountainous ridge, which was curving gently down into the water, was but a minute part of the endless ice mass covering the inland of Greenland. The blue-green caves at the waterline told him that the iceberg was not a great block of ice but, on the contrary, columns of ice crystals that time and frost had fused. Columns that would easily break from one another when the ice met the ocean current and was inundated with water.

Navarana had talked a lot about that barren universe of ice in the interior. Even though the Human Beings never visited the eternal glacier, as there were no game animals to be found there, the glacier was for her a powerful spirit in a vibrant old body. A being that also ruled over such mighty spirits as Pitoraq, the wild wind.

Earlier, Brendan had listened to all she told without particular interest. Now, with that gleaming mirror image filling him with a joy so intense that only love could create its equal, he understood what she meant. After that he watched the tiniest change in the landscape attentively, and he longed to know and understand more.

Brendan was glad that Navarana only watched but did not question. He could not even explain to himself what was happening.

Again, he asked God for guidance.

Lord, this land has now become my own. How do You wish me to live here in Your honor?

He did not actually expect an answer, since he now knew

that he had to find the answers for himself. It was only in his earlier life, when others had determined what he was to think and how he was to believe, that he had been given all the answers. Now he had to live with uncertainty and the giddy feeling of being the first from his own world to discover this foreign world.

Navarana worked diligently on the suits they were to be married in. Never had she been so meticulous in scraping and tanning and cutting leather. Never had she sewn more hope into any clothing than she did into his. She took extra pains with the anorak and mittens. She spent endless hours cutting hair-fine ribbons of salmon and lumpfish skin and dyeing the seal's gut with urine. But it was worth the effort, for the embroidery on the anorak and mittens turned out to be the most beautiful she had ever done. The high *kamiks* that she had so reluctantly sewn for him from the sow's pelt she kneaded until soft and adorned with double seams. As she sewed a new anorak for herself, following the design of women's costumes in the north, she thought more and more often of her sisters. She had decided that they should stay behind with the Grandmothers and the Old One. It was too dangerous to take them along on the great journey by sled, for not even she knew how it would end. There was no safer place for them than with the

Grandmothers, and she consoled herself in the certainty that they would learn and experience the most amazing things. Yet she was still bothered, for she knew that they had obediently done only what was best for her. What they most wanted was to follow her anywhere in the world, no matter how dangerous. She had seen it in their eyes: their sorrow over her leaving them behind and their fear that she would not come back. Maybe they had noticed her own fear over what awaited her at the end of the sled journey. A quest that more and more felt like a black abyss.

Her anorak was finished. It was wide, with long embroidered V-shaped points in front and back and a roomy hood.

"What's that for?" he asked curiously.

She blushed when she answered: "To carry our children in."

"Where are we going on our journey, Navarana? Won't you tell me what's in store for you?"

He had not asked before. He knew that the quest that the Grandmothers and the Old One had given her was enormous. He noticed that it made her increasingly uneasy.

"Sit still while I'm working." Her voice was tender. "It's not easy to fasten your beads to your headband. They're so much heavier than the shells we use."

It was Brendan who had suggested that she should use

the blue glass beads from his rosary. "I'll remember my prayers anyway," he said.

"There, you see, I'll soon be done, and your golden hair will no longer fall in your eyes when we're traveling and you'll be just as finely adorned as I."

He did not ask again. She would tell him everything when the time was right.

He was fully dressed and rejoiced at the sight of her. At the sight of her hands gathering her gleaming hair in a tight knot on her head and of her fingers' quick movements when the thongs with their shells were fastened around the knot of her hair. He never grew tired of seeing the tiny wrinkle in her forehead and her eyes smiling with their glint of gold.

"I'm ready," she said.

"I've been ready for an eternity."

They walked hand in hand down to the edge of the ice. There were no guests; the dogs sat quite still. There was no one to give them away to each other as bride and groom, but the whales soon came and soared into the air in a mighty double spiral of black and white and glittering foam, and the sky resounded with their whistling song.

In the faint sunshine they promised each other in their own languages eternal faithfulness.

He gave her his marvel of a stone, the stone with the fluttering life that was once frozen by time.

"Maybe all life really becomes stone and then is resurrected in sun." She held it up toward the sun, and the butterfly shone like her eyes.

She gave him her father's polar-bear claw, and he knew that he had received the greatest treasure she possessed.

Finally, she was prepared to tell him about her quest.

"We must journey to the edge of the world, where once upon a time the sun was born," she began. "There the sun will be resurrected if my power is strong enough. The rest Human Beings can manage for themselves. Human Beings will adjust to nature's changes, just as we always have had to do. But," she continued slowly, "no one can adjust to a world without sun, for she is the absolute sovereign of all life."

She grew silent.

"Tell me more, Navarana," begged Brendan. "I need to know everything about the dangers awaiting you and the evil you have to combat."

There was nothing he feared more than that she would disappear into her mysterious World of the Spirits, which he knew so little about.

She looked at him, surprised. "You're right; I've told you too little. Forgive me. The power I shall meet is terribly old and mighty, but the Raven is not just evil. It's true that he is a trickster and liar, but he can also be helpful to Human Beings. The Ancestors say the Raven was present when the world was created from earth and stone that fell from the sky. The Raven was in the world before Human Beings, for the First Human Being—who long lay huddled waiting to be born—met the Raven, saw that he raised his beak, and saw that beneath the raven mask there was a Human Being. No one knows for certain whether the Raven created the first light, but all know that he loves the sun and that he steals it when he can. The Ancestors have described how it happened the very first time.

"*In the beginning, when Human Beings came, there was only darkness. At that time a young woman was living with her father by the seashore. Once, when she was going to fetch some water, she saw a feather floating toward her from the sea. She opened her mouth and the feather floated in. She swallowed it and was with child. The child was born with a raven's beak, and the woman tried to find games for her child. There was a hunting float, a bladder blown full of air, hanging in her father's house, the kind of bladder that hunters fasten to a seal when it has been killed in order to keep it floating in the water. Her father had hidden the sun inside the bladder. The child, whom the woman called Raven, pointed to the bladder and cried. At last she let him have it, but he tore it to pieces, and immediately the dwelling was filled with light. When her father came home, he scolded her. But Raven had disappeared with the sun.*

"Since then the Raven and the Human Beings have fought over the sun," Navarana concluded. She smiled, and he saw how spent she was. "The Raven has hung the sun on the sky when he has felt like sharing it with others, and he has swallowed it when he's wanted it for himself."

It was a strange story. Completely different from the Bible's account of how God the Almighty created the world and arranged everything in it. Brendan burned with desire to ask her how it could be that the Raven was both present when the world was created and reborn as a Human Being. But this was not the time for questions. For now it was important just to console her in every way he could.

"Miracles occur when one's faith is strong," he said. "Your faith is solid as a rock, Navarana. You'll be victorious."

He could hear how hollow it sounded, but he would say and do whatever it took for her to retain her hope.

"Faith, hope, and dreams are not enough. You know that yourself," she said sadly.

She grew silent again.

"I don't know whether my power is strong enough to withstand the trials that are coming," she said finally. "I don't know what will happen if my strength fails. But I do know that if I lose, the harm will be irreparable. For me, for us, for everything and everyone."

He knew that she was seeking words to express that which was most difficult.

"Before you arrived, there was little I was actually afraid of. Now I fear losing the life that the two of us have just begun and the life that we still have not lived. The thought of all I don't want to lose has sapped my will. Can you understand that?"

Of course he understood. It was precisely what he himself could not bear to think about.

"You will not be alone," he said, and knew that his promise would be easy to keep.

SIXTEEN

They followed the route that Human Beings had wandered from time immemorial, first far to the north, then even farther toward the west. Finally they were to travel directly eastward, toward the sun's birthplace, where day lasted the whole summer and night lasted the whole winter.

They had journeyed long through a landscape that changed dramatically from rugged coast to naked inland plateaus, from areas of frozen torrents to woods of slender, white-clad birches. But the sky was still as gray as slate, and the sun was barely a pale shadow of itself.

Brendan was worried about Navarana. She neither saw nor heard anything around her. He tried to get her to see that wild storms no longer threatened and to notice that the cold smelled steadily stronger of the sea. He reminded her that the Sea's Mother did her utmost to keep hope alive, for each day she sent her chosen children to them. But it was as if Navarana had lost her belief in change. At the same time she drove herself and the dogs harder than ever before, and Brendan began to fear that she was going to overstrain both the dogs and them.

"Navarana," he said, "we've promised each other that nothing is to be hidden between us. Tell me what's bothering you."

"Nothing," she said quickly. Too quickly, and, ashamed, she sent him a sidelong glance.

They had arrived at one more abandoned settlement. Brendan saw that she had tears in her eyes as she explored the dwellings to figure out how long it had been since anyone had lived there. When she was finished, she sat down and stared into space.

"The Human Beings have set out to search for new places to fish and hunt, both on the coast and inland," Brendan said hopefully. "Perhaps they've already found one."

"Perhaps they're already dead," she answered somberly. "They and all the other Human Beings in the world."

He said no more, just rocked her slowly in his arms until she had finished telling him how frightened she was of meeting the Raven.

· · ·

After that the daily journeys by sled grew shorter and they used more of their time to grow closer to each other.

Slowly, Navarana regained her courage.

"It's not going to be as the Raven intended," said Brendan. "Aren't those your own words?"

She nodded. "Thank you, my best friend. Thank you for trusting me."

Finally they found life, and the dogs began to bark before they saw the settlement. There was no smoke coming from the dwellings. No one came out to meet them, and the dogs' harnesses lay empty in the snow. A kayak lay bottom-up on the rack, but it had a long slash on its underside that no one had bothered to repair.

There was misfortune here. A misfortune Navarana had seen all too often.

She hurried to the largest round dwelling and scrabbled down the entry without waiting for Brendan. It was dark inside, and the air was dense with sickness. But they were still alive, three women and five little children. The hearth was cold and the whale-oil lamp had been licked dry.

When Brendan came in, he immediately began to examine the sick, while Navarana lit the lamp and brought seal meat from the sled. They worked together as if their hands and thoughts belonged to one body, and they did not rest until the fever loosened its grip on the women and children.

After many days of warmth, food, and care, the women could tell their story.

There had been five large families at the settlement when the severe cold arrived. They were families that had lived together compatibly and shared winter settlement and summer camp for many generations. In all that time there had been an abundance of seal, fish, and birds on the hunting grounds and plenty of hare, ptarmigan, and reindeer in the mountains. Never had they experienced hunger. They had always had more than enough to barter with the Human Beings at the settlements in the north and south. No one had been prepared for the endless winter. No one believed that it was possible, until it was too late. By then all the stores of meat were gone, and the hunters had no choice but to brave the storms, against all common sense. One after the other, the hunters fell prey to death. At last, the families could no longer endure the exhausting wait. They packed everything they owned and left the settlement. Only the weakest remained, and they were without providers. They had agreed to face the end together.

"You shall have our women's boat," said Navarana, "and everything you'll need to manage until you find a new place to hunt. Just promise me to sing our songs."

At first they could not believe it. Then they refused to accept it.

But eventually they did as Navarana wished.

Brendan was horrified by their story. "It's unbelievable that a family could leave behind its women and children."

"Then you still do not understand how hard the circumstances are that we live in," she answered dryly. "These women were not forced. They chose to make the greatest of sacrifices for the sake of their families."

"But why didn't they accept immediately when you offered them life?"

"No one likes to owe his life to another."

"I ought to know that better than anyone else." He said it before she could.

"You must remember, they've lost everything except their pride."

Her voice was full of laughter when she continued. "But I owe you great thanks, since it was due to you that they were convinced. I said that you expected them to accept."

He looked questioningly at her, and she smiled apologetically.

"You're now a powerful shaman whom the Moon Man has sent. They've never seen a stranger before. Or one who is as colorless as the moon, as the eldest girl described you. It was then that I figured out the solution." She grew serious. "Forgive my misusing you, but nothing is more important than saving our children's lives."

He laughed into her hair.

"How good that my pale skin finally could be of use."

"It has long been giving joy, as you very well know, but it has also been of use."

She laid his hand on her stomach. Its soft curve had become slightly larger.

"Are you certain?"

She nodded.

"Holy Virgin Mary!" he exclaimed.

Then he knelt in the snow and thanked his Savior's Mother at length and with all his heart.

Navarana felt for the first time that she wanted to know about his spirits.

They waited until the women and children had rowed out of the bay with the women's boat.

Then he turned toward her and said quietly, "Are you ready?"

"Yes, never have I had more to fight for."

"Never have we," he merely said.

Then they started out on the last part of the journey.

SEVENTEEN

They reached the edge of the world just as darkness arrived.

The land that they had long been traveling through was flat, desolate, and windswept. The mist was so thick that they could scarcely see a hand in front of their faces and so heavy that all sounds were deadened. Before them, in the impenetrable darkness, Brendan could hear the rush of the ocean. It sounded eerie, as if the ocean lay at the bottom of a deep pit.

Brendan had been taught that at the edge of the world there was nothing. Now he knew that Nothing was hell on earth.

"We must find the dwelling of the Spirits," whispered

Navarana. She did not dare disturb the primeval silence. "I'll prepare myself to meet the Raven there."

Brendan began to shiver. He wanted to beg her not to do it after all, for he would die without her. But he seized her hand and accompanied her on the search.

It stood out on the edge, a long, large dwelling built of whalebone that shone like a specter in the dark mist.

"It's here that families from all parts of the Human Beings' great land come to celebrate winter's end. Here the shamans drum until dawn breaks and the sun rises," said Navarana.

"Are they also coming now?"

She nodded.

"Why can't we just wait until they come, why can't we?"

"Because the winter is *not* over, my friend. To make it end is precisely my mission."

They stood close to each other. Both thought about how strong they were together whenever one of them was weak.

They were silent as they fed the dogs and carried their gear into the Spirits' dwelling. They worked as calmly as usual, but both felt that it was perhaps for the last time.

When they had finished eating, Navarana said quietly, "Now is the moment. I'll call the Raven."

Brendan felt numb. He wanted to beg her to wait at least until it grew light, but he did not have the strength.

"Will you help me?" She was unable to meet his eyes.

"When I finish drumming, you must bind my hands and feet. I want to know that my body is lying quietly and safely with you while I'm traveling to meet the Raven."

"What else can I do?" He could scarcely hear his own voice.

She smiled sadly. "Trust me, and let the drum sound the whole night. Then I shall find the way back to the two of us."

The silky, soft voice slipped out of the empty darkness like a caressing tongue against her navel.

"I've been waiting for you, Navarana. How I've longed to have you."

She felt that ancient power, and for a moment she wanted to surrender herself.

"It's here you belong, for you and I are children of the same kin. That wretched foreigner, what has he to offer a woman like you?"

She became enraged. "You'll never have me, for I know your sly tricks and I remember all your evil deeds."

"Do you repudiate me? You whom I have rocked, whom I have flown in and out of. As if you were my own body. That you have surely told him?"

His laughter was evil, and she remembered that she must not lose her head.

"You're bragging, old man!" The icy voice scarcely

sounded like her own. "You've never dared to come near me, for you know that I would do as you do. I would entice you with all my openings and then devour you with all the teeth I have."

"So you have come to measure your strength against mine? And as for the miserable creature you are begetting bastards with, is he down on his knees praying to his god for you?"

Don't get angry! she thought. He's only waiting to trap you.

Aloud she said, "I'll put an end to your greed for power. You've stolen the sun for the last time."

Her voice was calm, but she was trembling.

It was ominously quiet for a while. Then the darkness turned a shimmering blue and she heard the dry rustling of feathers. The Raven slowly stepped forth. He spread his black wings and opened his head with its enormous red beak. She saw something white moving in the darkness beneath the raven shape. Like the pale shadow of a Human Being.

"Your Brendan has surely told you beautiful things about his Christian faith. But has he remembered to tell you what his actual task is in the Land of the Human Beings? Just hear what his shamans have commanded him to do."

The Raven suddenly changed, and the voice she heard was foreign and frightful:

Brother Brendan! You shall combat the Devil and all his works in Greenland. You shall Christianize all heathens, and those who refuse to bow down to the Almighty God you shall strike down without mercy. You are a soldier in the Holy War, Brendan. Your task is to annihilate all disbelievers and guard God's realm here on earth.

"You are evil!" she screamed.

"Was the truth too much for you?" The voice was soft as silk again. "Sweet Navarana, you know that I mean you no harm. I'm only showing you *their* evil and mania for power. The strangers tolerate no other gods than their own, and they are willing to kill in the name of their god."

"Brendan is no murderer!"

"Not yet, but the rest of his pack of foreigners are. You have naturally heard about how his father died? No? But ask him to tell you of his bravery when they burned his father alive," cackled the Raven.

She was speechless. No matter what she said or how hard she fought, he found something loathsome to surprise her with. She could not stand to hear more cruel things about Brendan. Perhaps it was hopeless. Then she heard the sow's voice, as distant as the sea it came from: *Have you forgotten why I gave you the power? You who would not accept what was destined to be?*

No, she had not forgotten. She was exhausted and afraid, but she would not give up. She squeezed the medicine pouch at her breast hard and felt her fingers grow wonderfully warm. Attack where he is weakest, she thought.

"Finally I see what you are, Raven." Her voice was hard with disdain. "A wholly common carrion bird that gorges on death and misfortune. The Oldest Songs relate that you are of divine lineage. I've always believed that you were present when the world was created. But I believe that the Ancestors were mistaken, for you don't possess the mercy or heart of a god. You're not a Human Being in bird shape either, for the only feeling you know is the pleasure of torturing others."

"Do you repudiate your faith?" His voice was cracked.

He was frightened. She was not.

"No, I just despise your sickly power hunger and your vanity. I believe in good. You are evil. I will drive you out of the Human Beings' faith."

It grew terribly quiet. She knew that she had to attack before he managed to devise some sort of revenge.

"If you are really a Human Being in raven feathers, surely you can show yourself. All I have seen beneath your guise is the shadow of a pale maggot."

He hesitated too long, and it was too late. She was no longer vulnerable.

"Tell me, Old Bird, why you abducted the sun and the moon."

He ruffled his feathers. "You who know the Oldest Songs know why."

"Tell me in your own words," she coaxed.

And he told:

The Human Being and the Raven returned to the sky after the reindeer had fled. And the Human Being said, "If nothing is done to prevent Human Beings from killing so many animals, they will continue until they have killed everything you have created. It is best that you take the sun from them, so that they remain in darkness. Then they will die." The Raven agreed to this and said, "You stay here, and I will go out to get the sun."

Navarana laughed triumphantly.

"I thought that it would probably be that song you would sing for me. The song in which you are free of guilt. But I know other songs about why you abducted the sun and the moon. Those songs are about your desire and greed."

"Do you deny that Human Beings harm the animals and nature?"

"No, but I refuse to believe that a Human Being would punish himself and all future generations with death. It's not true. It's not just, either. Therefore, I have come to bring the sun back, for our unborn children are innocent and they shall have the right to change the world."

He laughed, but the laughter could not conceal his rage over her having tricked him.

"I'm waiting for your answer," she said stubbornly.

It came hesitantly: "What will you give me?"

"You'll have a chance to show mercy. Then you can continue to hear songs in your honor."

"If I refuse?"

"Then I will destroy your songs," she said simply.

"Give me time to think about it," he mumbled.

"You'll have time, but only until tomorrow. Then you'll meet Human Beings in a Song Contest for the sun."

Navarana used the rest of the night to call them together. They came from far and near, the shamans, women, children, and hunters. They came across ice, through the air, and by water—in sleds, kayaks, and women's boats. Before dawn they were all there, and Navarana was looking forward to the Song Contest for the sun. Everything was ready for the Raven's arrival. The women lit the whale-oil lamps, which were soon shining like the stars in the sky.

It was only Brendan whom Navarana was worried about.

He had watched and waited and drummed for her. She had wanted to tell him all about her victory over the Raven. She had not considered what he might feel about all the evil things the Raven had said. But by the time she understood how thoughtless she had been, the harm was irreparable and Brendan was beside himself with shame.

His words, when he finally began to speak, came in fits and starts, as if each one was torture: "I was there when they led my father to the pyre. I saw the fire lick greedily around him and the stake. I heard the hate-filled shouts, 'Burn the heretic!' and I scrambled away from the square. Yes, I fled. I was five years old and terrified that they would burn me too."

He did not care what she thought. He just cried as he had not cried since the day he fled from his father's execution.

She rocked him for a long time and whispered, "I have humiliated you before, but never like this. Can you forgive me, my friend?"

"I would have told you myself. One day. When the wound no longer ached."

"Let us drum and travel together," she begged. "There's still time before dawn."

"I don't have the strength, Navarana. I am too loathsome."

"Your self-contempt only you can fight, and you have time enough for that. But I can help you fly, for you need to see what we must win back."

. . .

And they flew. Above the ancient inland ice, above the mighty mountain ranges bathed in light and the green plateaus mottled with trotting reindeer, above silver water that turned to dripping gold when the birds soared, and above glaciers brightly gliding toward the edge of the world.

She flew above and below him and through him, and she whispered, "She'll inherit all this, and she'll know how to do what is right for her world."

He folded his wings about her. "Do you know what to name her?"

"She'll receive many names, for she'll be loved by all. My name for her is Akaia, the very first."

When they returned, the Song Contest was under way, and the Raven danced and sang against them all. Never had Navarana heard such drumming and never anything to equal the songs. There were songs about hatred and bitterness, but also about forgiveness and joy. There were telling songs about the Raven's vanity, but also about Human Beings' foolishness. She had expected that the Song Contest would go on for a long time before the Raven finally submitted, but she saw that he had already hung the sun in place on the horizon.

He continued singing, just to be certain that they remembered the songs about him.

They promised never to forget the songs.

Then it grew silent as the sun rose and the world turned.

Brendan and Navarana turned their sled around and hurried back. The sun rose ever higher. It would not leave the sky. It glowed day and night as they traveled, and they rejoiced in the changes. They saw the sea open and heard the icebergs sailing. They saw flocks of eider ducks rocking on the waves and heard the hunting screeches of the hungry gulls. They saw the musk oxen trot across the plateaus with their winter coats waving about them like tattered wings, and finally they heard the dogs barking and Navarana's sisters shouting with joy.

They were alone, the Grandmothers and her sisters. The Old One had remained behind with the Raven.

"It's nothing to mourn over." Aanaa the Eldest smiled. "We know where he is and that he delights in the endless Song Contests with the Raven."

"We've received all his songs," said Navarana's sisters.

They had received much more, Navarana noticed. They had learned to take care of themselves.

She began to prepare herself for Akaia's arrival.

Brendan was preparing for something else, which he did not talk about for some time.

"Are you leaving?" she finally dared to ask.

"Leaving?" He looked at her, surprised. "Wherever to?"

"Home. Where you came from."

"This is my home," he answered, continuing to tan the seal gut. "Just wait a little, then I'll show you, Navarana."

But then she saw it for herself. He was preparing a skin to write on.

"May I learn?"

He laughed and his blue eyes shone. "I have prepared enough for you and the book."

She looked questioningly at him.

"I must write down the whole story," he said seriously. "I don't want to forget any part of all that has happened or to conceal anything. There's much that I have not had the courage to tell you. Things that not even the Raven knows. But they are tales too dark even in the light of the midnight sun."

She continued to hunt and sew and play and sing songs for Akaia.

Meanwhile he wrote a tale that was for her and him and for all people of all sorts, but most of all for the future.

He had been transformed in the Land of the Human Beings. But nothing had changed in the world he came from. One day they would come again, fortune hunters, explorers, conquerors, and missionaries. He was quite sure of it, for he was of their kin and knew what they thought and believed. Therefore, he wrote about his own great dream. About Brendan's journey of transformation. Perhaps people from his world would one day come with curiosity and respect. Not with disdain and the sword.

He wrote and hoped.

There was nothing he could do but hope.

The rest people would have to manage for themselves.